ADIÓS HEMINGWAY

ADIÓS HEMINGWAY

Leonardo Padura Fuentes

Translated from the Spanish by
John King

CANONGATE
Edinburgh · New York · Melbourne

First published in Great Britain in 2005 by
Canongate Books Ltd., Edinburgh, Scotland

Printed in the United States of America

FIRST AMERICAN PAPERBACK EDITION

ISBN-10: 1-84195-795-X
ISBN-13: 978-1-84195-795-1

Canongate
841 Broadway
New York, NY 10003

Distributed by Publishers Group West

www.groveatlantic.com

06 07 08 09 10   10 9 8 7 6 5 4 3 2 1

This novel, like those before it and those still to come, is dedicated to Lucía, with love.

It was not always hot where the dead lay;
often the rain bathed them when they were on top of
the earth and softened it when they buried them in it
and at times the rain carried on until it was all mud
and uncovered them and they had to bury them again.

Ernest Hemingway,
'A Natural History of the Dead'

AUTHOR'S NOTE

In the Autumn of 1989, as a hurricane was devastating Havana, Inspector Conde solved his final case as an active member of the CID. Having made up his mind to become a writer, he handed in his resignation the day he turned thirty-six and received the dreadful news that one of his oldest friends had started to go through the administrative process needed to leave Cuba. That story of Mario Conde's last detective adventure appears in the novel *Autumn Landscape*, ending the 'Four Seasons' cycle that also includes *Perfect Tense*, *Lent Winds* and *Masks*, written between 1990 and 1997.

Resolved to leave Conde for a time, I began to write a novel in which he did not appear. While in the midst of that other story, my Brazilian publishers asked me to contribute to their series

'Literature or Death' and, if I accepted, to let them know the name of the writer around whom the story would revolve. After very little thought the project caught my imagination, and the writer who came into my mind straightaway was Ernest Hemingway, with whom I have had a fierce love–hate relationship for years. However, as I looked for a way of coming to terms with my dilemma with the author of *The Sun Also Rises*, the best solution that occurred to me was to transfer my obsessions onto Conde – as I had done on so many other occasions – and turn him into the protagonist of the story.

The relationship between Hemingway and Conde, and the moment a corpse makes its mysterious appearance in the Havana house belonging to the North American writer, developed into this novel that, in every sense, must be read as such: because it is just a novel and many of the events narrated in it, even when they have been drawn from the most ascertainable reality and the strictest chronology, are filtered through fiction and mingled with it to the extent that, at the present moment, I'm incapable of telling where one ends and the other begins. However, although some characters keep their real names, others have been re-baptised in order to avoid damaging possible sensitivities, and the figures from reality mix with those from fiction in a territory that is ruled only by the laws and time of the novel. In this way, the Hemingway of this work is, naturally, a Hemingway of fiction, since the story in which he finds himself involved is just a product of my imagination, and in the writing of which I even indulge in the poetic and postmodern licence of hinting at some passages from his works and interviews in order to construct the story of that long night of 2/3 October 1958.

Finally, I would like to give grateful thanks for the help that I have received from people such as Francisco Echevarría, Danilo Arrate, María Caridad Valdés Fernández and Belkis Cedeño, specialists at the Finca Vigía Museum; all of them Cuban Hemingway fanatics. Thanks also to my invaluable readers Alex Fleites, Jose Antonio Michelena, Vivian Lechuga, Stephen Clark, Elizardo Martínez

and the real and authentic John Kirk, as well as to
my wife Lucía López Coll.

L.P.F

Mantilla, Summer 2000

First he spat, then he expelled the remainder of the smoke from deep within his lungs and finally he threw the tiny cigarette butt into the water, flicking it with his fingers. The burning sensation on his skin brought him back to reality, and, once back in the world, he thought how much he would have liked to know the real reason for his being here, looking out to sea, preparing to undertake an unpredictable journey into the past. He then began to convince himself that many of the questions he would have to ask would have no answers; but it reassured him to remember how it had been the same with many other questions that had pursued him throughout his life, and he accepted the gloomy fact that he was going to have to live with more doubts than certainties. Perhaps that was why he was no longer a policeman, he said to himself, as he put another cigarette between his lips.

The pleasant breeze coming from the little cove proved to be a blessing in the midst of the summer heat, but Mario Conde had chosen that short stretch of seafront, shaded by some ancient casuarina trees, for reasons connected with neither the sun nor the heat. Sitting on the wall, with his feet dangling down towards the rocks, he enjoyed the sensation of freedom from the tyranny of time, imagining how good it would be to spend the rest of his life in that exact spot, devoting his time just to thinking, reminiscing and watching the calm, peaceful sea. And if a good idea occurred to him he might even start writing, since in his personal paradise Conde had turned the sea, with its smells and sounds, into the perfect setting for his spirit. There abided, fixed in his imagination like a tenacious shipwrecked sailor, the sweet image of himself living in a wooden house, looking out over the sea, given over to writing in the mornings and to fishing and swimming in the afternoons. Reality had been battering this dream for some years now

with typical fervour, and Conde couldn't understand why he still clung to the image, which had
been so vivid and photographic at first, but from
whose rather poor impressionist palette he could
now barely make out the lighter patches or faded
brightness.

So he stopped trying to find an explanation
for that afternoon: he just knew that he had had to
return to that little cove at Cojímar so grounded
in his memory. In fact, everything had begun in that
very place, facing the same sea, beneath the same
casuarina trees, amongst the same old indelible
smells, that day in 1960 when he had encountered
Ernest Hemingway. The exact date eluded him (as
had so many good things in life) and he couldn't be
sure if he had still been five or if he was already
six, although at the time his grandfather Rufino
was already taking him along to the most varied of
places, from cockpits and the bars in the port, to
the domino tables and the baseball stadiums – those
cherished spots where Conde had learnt some of
the most important things a man must know. That
unforgettable afternoon they had watched some

cockfights in Guanabacoa, and his grandfather, who had won his bets, as he usually did, decided to reward them by taking young Mario to visit the small town of Cojímar, so that he could have what he insisted was the best ice cream in Cuba, made by the Chinaman Casimiro Chon, with fresh fruit in old wooden sorbet bowls.

Conde thought that he could still remember the creamy taste of the *mamey* fruit ice cream, and his delight in watching the manoeuvres of a beautiful yacht with a black hull and brown woodwork, from which two huge fishing-rods stuck out skywards, making it look like an amphibious insect. If his memory was accurate, Conde had watched the yacht as it gently approached the shore, making its way between the flotilla of dilapidated fishing-boats anchored in the cove and dropping its anchor next to the jetty. At that moment a reddish-haired, shirtless man jumped from the yacht onto the concrete quay, caught hold of the rope that another man, hidden beneath a dirty white cap, threw to him from the vessel. Pulling on the end of the rope the red-haired man pulled the yacht up to a post and moored it there with a perfect knot. Perhaps his grandfather Rufino pointed something out to him, but Conde's eyes and memory had already fixed upon the other person – the man wearing the cap – who wore round-framed glasses with green lenses and had a thick, grey beard. He watched him as he jumped ashore and paused to say something to the man already standing on the quayside. Conde would live with the belief that he had seen how the two men shook hands and, without letting go, spoke for a while – perhaps a minute, perhaps even an hour – he couldn't remember. Then the old man with the beard embraced the other and, without casting a glance behind him, went along the quay towards the shore. There was something of Santa Claus in that old, rather dirty-bearded man with his large hands and feet; he walked with assurance, but somehow sadness emanated from him. Or perhaps it was just an unfathomable, magnetic premonition, foretelling the nostalgia lying in wait in a future that the boy could not even imagine.

When the man with the grey beard climbed

the concrete steps and reached the pavement, Conde saw how he tucked his cap under his arm. He took a small plastic comb from his shirt pocket and started to smooth down his hair, combing it backwards over and over again, as if this repeated action were essential. For a moment the man was so close to Conde and his grandfather that Conde caught a whiff of his smell: a mixture of sweat and the sea, of petrol and fish, an unhealthy, engulfing stench.

'Deteriorating rapidly.'

His grandfather had said this, but Conde had never figured out if he had been referring to the man or the weather, for at that stage in his recollection what he remembered and what he'd been told later became confused, the man walking past him and thunder heard from afar. So Conde usually cut off the reconstruction of his only encounter with Ernest Hemingway at that point.

'That's Hemingway, the American writer,' added his grandfather after the man had walked past. 'He likes cockfights too.'

Conde imagined turning the remark over in

his mind as he watched the writer walking over to a shiny black Chrysler parked on the other side of the street, and from the car window, without taking off his green-lensed glasses, he seemed to wave goodbye to him and his grandfather, although perhaps he extended his farewell much further than them, to the cove with the yacht and the red-haired man whom he had hugged, or to the Spanish watchtower constructed to defy the passage of time, or perhaps even at the furthest part of the Gulf Stream . . . But the boy had already caught the farewell gesture in mid-air and, before the car moved off, he returned it with his hand and voice.

'Adiós, Hemingway,' he shouted, and received in reply a smile from the man. Some years later, when he himself discovered the painful need to write and began to choose his literary idols, Mario Conde knew that that had been Ernest Hemingway's last trip across a stretch of sea that he had loved like few other places in the world, and he understood that the American writer could not have been saying goodbye to him, a tiny insect that had landed on the sea front at Cojímar, but that he had at that moment been bidding farewell to several of the most important things in his life.

'Want another?' asked Manolo.

'OK,' replied Conde.

'A double or a single?'

'What do you think?'

'Cachimba, two double rums,' shouted Inspector Manuel Palacios, with one arm raised, addressing the barman who began to serve the drink without removing the pipe from his mouth. The Watchtower wasn't a clean bar, let alone well-lit, but there was rum, silence and few drunkards, and from his table Conde could carry on watching the sea and the worn stones of the colonial tower to which the place owed its grand-sounding name. Unhurriedly, the barman walked over to their table, placed the drinks on it, and collected the empty glasses, picking them up between his dirty-nailed fingers, and looked at Manolo.

'Who the fuck do you think you are?' he said, slowly, 'I don't believe a word about you being a policeman.'

'For God's sake, Cachimba, don't get so fucking worked up,' said Manolo, trying to calm him down. 'I was only joking.'

The barman glared at him and moved away. He had already looked at Mario with loathing when he had asked him if they served a 'Papa Hemingway' there, the daiquiri the writer used to drink, made of two measures of rum, lemon juice, a few drops of maraschino and a lot of finely-crushed ice, but no sugar at all. ('The last time I saw a piece of ice was when I was a penguin,' the barman had replied.)

'So how did you know I was here?' Conde asked his former colleague after knocking back half his drink in one go.

'I'm not a cop for nothing, am I?'

'Don't steal my lines.'

'They're no good to you now, Conde . . . you're not a cop any longer,' said Inspector Manuel Palacios with a smile. 'It's quite simple. I know you so well, I expected you to be here. I don't know how many times you've told me that story about the day you saw Hemingway. Did he really wave goodbye to you, or is that something you made up?'

'You find out, that's what you're a cop for.'

'You pissed off with me?'

'Don't know. I just don't want to get involved in this . . . but at the same time I *do* want to get involved.'

'Listen, you get as involved in it as you want, and when you want to, walk away. After all, there's not much point to it anyway. It's almost forty years since . . .'

'I don't know why the hell I agreed to it . . . but then, I couldn't help myself even if I'd wanted to.'

Conde finished his drink, feeling sorry for himself. Eight years out of the police force is a long time and he would never have imagined it would be so easy to return to the fold. Recently, as he supposedly spent time writing, or at least trying to write, he had found himself spending much of the day buying old books all over the city in order to supply the bookstall of a dealer friend of his from whom he received 50 per cent of the profits.

Although the business was not that profitable, Conde liked the job for its peculiar advantages; he enjoyed the personal stories concealed behind the decision to get rid of a library that might have been built up over three or four generations, and he liked the time lapse between purchase and sale, during which he could read anything he liked as it passed through his hands. The essential drawback of the business operation, however, was evident when Conde suffered small cuts to his skin when he handled good old books damaged, at times irreparably, by carelessness and ignorance or when, instead of taking certain tempting volumes to his friend's bookstall, he decided to keep them in his own bookcase, an incurable symptom of the terrible infirmity of bibliophilia. But that morning, the day after a fierce summer storm, when his former colleague had phoned him and told him the story of the dead body discovered at Finca Vigía and offered to hand the investigation over to him if he wanted it, a visceral reaction had forced Conde to look painfully at the blank sheet of paper in his prehistoric Underwood typewriter and agree, even though he'd barely heard the first details of the case.

That summer storm had also lashed the district where Conde lived. Unlike hurricanes, these ferocious downpours, gales and flashes of lightning could arrive with no prior warning at any time in the afternoon to perform a swift, macabre dance over parts of the island. Their power, capable of devastating banana plantations and over-running drains, very rarely did any greater damage, but this particular storm had shown no mercy on Finca Vigía, once Hemingway's Havana home. It tore some of the tiles from the roof, cut off the electricity, demolished part of the fence around the courtyard and brought down an ancient, dying mango tree which had certainly been there before the building of the house back in 1905. Among the tree's exposed roots there had emerged some bones, which the experts had quickly identified as belonging to a man, Caucasian, about sixty years old, with the first signs of arthritis and an old, badly-healed fracture of the patella. He seemed to have been killed thirty or forty years ago, probably the late '50s, by two shots, almost certainly from a rifle. He had received one of the shots in the chest, seemingly through the right side, which, in addition to going through several of his vital organs, had severed his sternum and his vertebral column. The other bullet seemed to have entered his body through his abdomen, since it had fractured a rib in the dorsal area. Two shots fired from a powerful weapon, apparently at close range, causing the death of a man who, now, was nothing more than a bag of crumbling bones.

'Do you know why you agreed?' Manolo asked him, with a satisfied glance. Then, going cross-eyed, 'because a sonofabitch will always be a sonofabitch, however much he goes to confession and attends church. Once a cop, always a cop. That's why, Conde.'

'Why don't you tell me something useful instead of all that shit? With the information I've got, I can't even start to –'

'Because there isn't anything else and I doubt there will be either. It was forty years ago, Conde.'

'Be straight with me, Manolo . . . who cares anything about this case?'

'You really want to know? As things stand, just you, the dead man, Hemingway and I don't think anyone else . . . Look, as far as I'm concerned it couldn't be clearer. Hemingway had a filthy temper. One day someone fucked him around too much and he let him have two shots. Then he buried him. Nobody had any interest in the dead man at the time. Then Hemingway shot himself in the head and that was an end to the story. I called you up because I knew it would interest you and I want to leave an interval before closing the case. When I close it and the news gets out, the story of a dead man buried at Hemingway's house is going to make headlines halfway around the world . . .'

'And naturally, they're going to say that Hemingway killed him. And if it wasn't him, who did kill him?'

'That's what you're going to find out. If you can . . . Look, Conde, I'm up to here with work,' he said as he brought his hand up to his eyebrows. 'Things here are getting bloody nasty: every day there are more hold-ups, cases of embezzlement, muggings, prostitution, pornography . . .'

'Pity I'm not a cop any more. I love pornography.'

'Shut up Conde: pornography involving children.'

'This country's gone crazy . . .'

'That doesn't sound like you . . . Do you think I've got time to investigate Hemingway's life, someone who killed himself a thousand years ago, to find out if he's guilty or innocent?'

Conde smiled and looked out at the sea.

'Know something, Manolo? I would love to find out that it was Hemingway who killed that guy. That bastard has been getting up my nose for years. But it pisses me off to think they might land him with a murder he didn't commit. That's why I'm going to look into it . . . Have they already fully searched the place where they found the body?'

'Not yet, but tomorrow Crespo and Greco are going over there. We couldn't let any old labourer do it.'

'And what are you going to do?'

'Carry on with my work and within a week, when you tell me what you've found out, I'll close the case and forget this story and let someone else carry the can.'

Conde looked out to sea again. He knew that Inspector Palacios was right, but he felt strangely uncomfortable about it. Is it because I was a cop for too long? he wondered. And now I'm trying to be a writer, he thought, so as not to forget his true ambition.

'Come here, I want you to see something,' Conde said as he stood up. Without waiting for Manolo he crossed the road and went over to the small park where, under a canopy, there was a stone pedestal with a bronze bust. The light of the sun, slanting as it set, cast its final rays upon the green, almost smiling face of the man immortalised there.

'When I started writing, I imitated him. That guy was very important for me,' said Conde, staring at the sculpture.

Of all the tributes, invocations and commemorations of Hemingway that existed in Cuba, only this bust seemed tangible and real to him, like one of those simple affirmative clauses that Hemingway learnt to write in his old days as a reporter for the

Kansas City Star. To him, it seemed excessive and even unliterary that a marlin fishing competition should survive, invented by the writer himself and carried on after his death, still bearing the authority of his name. He considered phoney and tasteless (actually, disgusting) the 'Papa Doble' that he had once drunk at the Floridita, which had cost him money he could ill afford – a concoction that Hemingway had insisted – for medical reasons, of all things – on drinking without the saving grace of the spoonful of sugar that could have made the difference between a good cocktail and a rum baptised with too little water. More than tacky, he considered offensive the development of a glamorous Marina Hemingway designed to exclude the scruffy Cuban but enable the rich and beautiful of the world to enjoy yachts, beaches, meals, obliging whores and lots of skin-flattering sun. Even the Finca Vigía Museum, which he had stopped visiting years ago, seemed to him like a stage-set devised in life to commemorate death. In short, only the decaying and deserted square in Cojímar with its bronze bust felt real to him: it was the first posthumous tribute paid to the writer anywhere in the world, and it was the one that his biographers always forgot to mention. But it was the only sincere one, since it had been erected by the poor fishermen of Cojímar with their own money after they had scoured Havana for the bronze for the sculptor, who hadn't charged for his work either. Those fishermen, to whom in hard times Hemingway had given what he caught in favourable waters; to whom he had given well-paid work when they filmed *The Old Man and The Sea*; with whom he had drunk beer and rum that he paid for, and to whom he listened, in silence, as they spoke of huge fish caught in the warm waters of the great Gulf Stream – they felt what nobody else in the world could feel. For them a comrade had died, and that was something Hemingway was not even for other writers, journalists, bull fighters or white hunters in Africa, or even for the Spanish militiamen or those French resistance fighters at whose head he had entered Paris to carry out the alcoholic, euphoric liberation of the Ritz Hotel from Nazi occupation . . . That piece of bronze stood out against all the spectacular falsehood of Hemingway's life, the one true element among the myths that overcame the lies, and Conde admired the tribute not on account of the writer, who would never know of it, but for those men who had conceived it, with an honest intent that is rarely seen.

'And you know the worst thing about it?' added the former cop, 'I think he still is important to me.'

If Miss Mary had been at home that Wednesday night, they would have had dinner guests, as they did every Wednesday night, and he wouldn't have been able to drink so much wine. There probably wouldn't have been many guests because of late he tended to prefer peace and quiet and the conversation of a couple of friends to the alcoholic binges of previous times, especially since his liver had sounded a warning call on account of the quantity of alcohol he had consumed over the years; both drink and food featured at the top of a horrible list of prohibitions that was growing relentlessly. Still, Wednesday dinners at Finca Vigía were kept up as a ritual, and of all the people with whom he was acquainted, he preferred to share them with his old friend from the Spanish Civil War, Doctor Ferrer Machuca, and with the disturbing Valerie Danby-Smith, that gentle red-haired Irish girl who was so young and whom he had turned into his assistant so as not to fall in love with her, being convinced that matters of business and love should not be combined.

The sudden departure of his wife for the US to speed up the purchase of some land in Ketchum had left him alone, and at least for a few days he wanted to make the most of the sharp, unfamiliar feeling of solitude that so symptomised his old age. Each morning he got up with the sun and, as in the good old days, worked hard and well, standing before his typewriter and producing more than three hundred words a day, despite the fact that the truth that he was pursuing in the slippery story he had entitled *The Garden of Eden* seemed more and more elusive. Although he couldn't admit as much to anyone, the fact was that he had gone back to this project, conceived ten years before as a short story but now grown beyond his control, because he had had to stop work on updating *Death in the Afternoon.* As he'd been working on the old chronicle, devoted to the art and philosophy of bullfighting and in need of a thorough revision for the planned new edition, he had felt that his brain was functioning too slowly and on more than one occasion he had had to make an effort to remember details and even to consult some text about bullfighting in order to clarify certain points about that world which he had discovered in his prolonged love affair with Spain.

On the morning of Wednesday, 2 October 1958 he managed to write three hundred and seventy words and by midday he had been swimming, though he didn't keep track of the number of lengths covered so he wouldn't be ashamed by the ridiculous figures he achieved now – so much less than the mile that he used to swim every day even three or four years back. After lunch, he ordered his driver to take him to Cojímar, where he would have a chat with his old friend Ruperto, the skipper of the *Pilar*, and let him know of his intention to set out for the Gulf the following weekend, and give his exhausted brain a rest. Overcoming temptation, he got back home at dusk without stopping off first at the Floridita, a bar he was incapable of entering for just one drink.

He tucked into two swordfish steaks, covered with slices of onion, and a big plate of vegetables dressed just with lime juice, and at nine o'clock he asked Raúl to clear the table, close the windows and, when he had finished, go home – but first to bring up the bottle of Chianti he had been given the previous week. With lunch he had preferred a light, fragrant Valdepeñas, and his palate now needed the dry, virile taste of the Italian wine.

When he got up from the table he noticed a movement at the front door and saw Calixto's dark head appear. It always amazed him that despite being older than him and having spent fifteen years in prison, Calixto didn't have a single grey hair on his head.

'Can I come in, Ernesto?' the man asked. Hemingway beckoned him in. Calixto walked over and looked at him. 'How are you today?'

'Fine, I guess,' gesturing towards the empty bottle on the table.

'Delighted to hear it.'

Calixto was the most ubiquitous employee at the Finca, since he carried out the most varied tasks. He was just as happy working with the gardener as covering for the driver when he was on holiday; he also worked with the carpenter or spent his time painting the walls of the house. These days, at the insistence of Miss Mary – as everyone, including her husband, called her – he was in charge of the night security of the Finca with the responsibility of not leaving his boss alone in that huge house. If that order was not confirmation that they thought of him as an old man, then what the hell was it? He and Calixto had known each other for almost thirty years, ever since the days when Calixto smuggled alcohol into Key West and Joe Russell bought it from him. They often drank together in Sloppy Joe's and in Hemingway's house at Key West, and he enjoyed hearing the tough Cuban's stories of how, during the Prohibition years, he had crossed the Straits of Florida more than two hundred times to get Cuban rum into the southern states of America. Then they didn't see each other for a long time, though when he began to visit Havana, Hemingway found that Calixto was in prison for having killed a man during a drunken brawl in a bar on the quayside. When he got out of prison, in 1947, they had met by chance at the door of the Floridita, and, when he heard about all Calixto's problems, Hemingway offered him work, without the faintest idea what kind of work he could give him. Since that moment, Calixto had roamed around his property, determined to do something useful to justify his wages and the favour he owed his writer friend.

'I'm going to have a coffee. Shall I pour you one?' asked Calixto, moving off towards the kitchen.

'No, not today. I'll carry on drinking wine.'

'Don't overdo it, Ernesto,' he said from the next room.

'I won't overdo it. And you can go to hell with your reformed drunkard's advice . . .'

Calixto came back into the drawing-room, with a cigarette between his lips. He smiled as he talked to his boss.

'In the good old days in Key West I always used to knock you out. Or have you already forgotten that?'

'Nobody remembers about that any more. Least of all me.'

'Well, I'm off now. I'll take a cup of coffee with me,' he said. 'Shall I do the rounds?'

'No, I'll do it.'

'See you later?'

'Sure. See you later.'

If Miss Mary had been at home, after the meal and conversation, he would have read a few pages from some book – perhaps the Argentinian edition of *The Liver and its Illnesses* by a certain H.P. Himsworth, which described liver ailments and their distressing consequences in brutal terms – while he drank his one permitted glass of wine, usually left over from the meal. Miss Mary would play canasta with Ferrer and Valerie, while he, a silent presence, enjoyed his sideways view of Valerie, whom Mary had cleverly taken off with her, arguing that she needed her help for certain legal and banking business she had to carry out in New York. When all's said and done, an old leopard doesn't change its spots . . . After drinking the wine and reading for a while he wouldn't have stayed up long: he would have soon said goodnight to the three of them, as they all knew that it had become his habit to go to bed at about eleven o'clock, whether he was doing the rounds of the Finca or not . . . So much routine, repetition, habits that were taken for granted, foreseeable actions; they all seemed to him the most incontrovertible indicator of his state of old age, but he found it enjoyable to deceive himself with a feeling of responsibility towards literature that he had not felt since those distant days in Paris, when he didn't know who would publish his books or who would read them, and he fought for each word as if his very life were at stake.

'Here's your wine, Papa.'

'Thanks, son.'

Raúl Villaroy placed the uncorked bottle and the clean, crystal glass on top of the small bar next to the armchair. Even though he had served him since 1941, shortly after Hemingway had taken up residence in the house with his third wife, Raúl would never have dared to say anything to him about the wine and Hemingway knew that he wouldn't let the cat out of the bag to Miss Mary. Raúl's loyalty was as absolute as that of Calixto, but with a devoted dog-like quality that made it calmer and more reserved. Of all his employees, Raúl was the one he loved most and the only one who, when he called him 'Papa', said it as if he really was his father.

'Papa, are you sure you want to spend another night alone here?'

'Yes, Raúl, don't worry. Have the cats been fed?'

'Yes, Dolores took them their fish, and I fed the dogs. Black Dog was the only one who didn't want to eat; he seems on edge. A moment ago he was barking back there. I went down to the swimming pool, but I didn't see anyone.'

'I'll give him something. He always eats when I feed him.'

'That's true, Papa.'

Raúl picked up the bottle and half-filled the wine glass. Hemingway had taught him to leave it open for a few minutes before pouring, to let the wine breathe and settle.

'Who's going to do the rounds?'

'I'll do it. I've already told Calixto.'

'Do you really want me to go off and leave you alone?'

'Yes, Raúl, that's fine. If I need you I'll call.'

'Mind you do call me. But I'll have a look around later anyway.'

'You're as bad as Miss Mary . . . Don't you worry, I'm not a helpless old man.'

'I know that Papa. OK, sleep well. Tomorrow I'll be here at six o'clock for breakfast.'

'What about Dolores? Why can't she prepare it? She usually does.'

'If Miss Mary's away, I should be here.'

'That's fine, Raúl. Good night.'

'Good night, Papa. Is the wine all right?'

'It's great.'

'That's good. I'm off now. Good night, Papa.'

'Good night, Raúl.'

That Chianti really did have a great taste. It was a present from Adriana Ivancich, the Venetian countess with whom he had fallen in love a few years back and whom he had turned into Renata in *Across the River And Into the Trees*. Drinking it reminded him of how the young girl's lips tasted, and that comforted him and eased the feeling of guilt at drinking more than was advisable.

If you want to carry on living, cut out drinking and adventures, Ferrer and the other doctors had warned him. He had problems with his blood pressure, his cholesterol level was high, his incipient diabetes could get worse, his liver and kidneys hadn't recovered after he was injured in those plane crashes in Africa, and his sight and hearing were going to deteriorate if he didn't look after himself: such a collection of illnesses and restrictions was what he was being reduced to. And what about bullfights? Fine, but in moderation. He had to return to the bullring; he needed to get back to bullfights and their atmosphere for the re-write of *Death in the Afternoon* which was turning out to be so difficult. He downed the whole glass and poured himself some more. The sound of the red wine pouring into the glass conjured up something he couldn't quite remember, although it was connected with one of his adventures. What the hell can it be? he wondered, and the horrible realisation dawned on him, familiar, though he tried not to think about it: with no more adventures or memories, what would he write about?

His biographers and critics always insisted on emphasising his taste for danger, war, extreme situations – in short, for adventure. Some of them considered him a man-of-action-turned-writer, others thought him a clown in search of exotic or dangerous settings that would add impact to what he wrote. But they had all played their part in mythologising, either through praise or criticism, a life that they all agreed he had forged with his actions across half the globe. The truth, as usual, was more complicated and awful: without my life story I wouldn't have been a writer, he said to himself, and looked at his wine against the light, without drinking it. He knew that his imagination had always been limited and unreliable, and merely recounting the things that he had seen and learnt about in life had allowed him to write in a way that exuded the veracity he demanded of literature. Without the bohemian experience in Paris and the bullfights he wouldn't have written *The Sun Also Rises*. Without the wounds received at Fossalta, the hospital in Milan and his desperate love for Agnes von Kurosowsky, he would never have had the idea for *A Farewell to Arms*. Without the safari in 1934 and the bitter taste of fear he experienced in his close encounter with a wounded buffalo, he wouldn't have written *Green Hills of Africa*, or two of his best stories, 'The Short Happy Life of Francis Macomber' and 'The Snows of Kilimanjaro'. Without Key West, the *Pilar*, Sloppy Joe's and smuggled alcohol, *To Have and Have Not* wouldn't have been born. Without the war in Spain and the bombing raids and heartless Martha Gellhorn, he would never have written *The Fifth Column* and *For Whom the Bell Tolls*. Without the Second World War and without Adriana Ivancich *Across the River And Into the Trees* wouldn't exist. Without all those days devoted to the Gulf and without the marlin that he caught and without the stories of other huge marlin that he had heard the fishermen of Cojímar talking about, *The Old Man and the Sea* would never have seen the light of day. Without the 'Crooks' Factory' that went with him to hunt for Nazi submarines, without Finca Vigía, and without the Floridita and the drinks he'd consumed and the characters he'd met there, he wouldn't have written *Islands in the Stream*. And what about *A Moveable Feast*? And *Death in the Afternoon*? And what about the 'Nick Adams' short stories? And this *Garden of Eden* that was refusing to flow as it should and dragging on and getting lost? He had to forge a life for himself in order to forge a literature; he had to fight, kill, fish, live, in order to be able to write.

'No, for fuck's sake, I didn't invent a life for myself,' he said aloud, and he didn't like the sound of his own voice in the midst of so much silence. He drained his glass.

With the bottle of Chianti beneath his arm and the glass in his hand, he walked over to the window of the drawing-room and looked out at the garden and the night. He strained his eyes, almost until they hurt, trying to see into the darkness, just as those African cats did. Something must exist, beyond what can be foreseen, beyond what is obvious; something that could lend some charm to the final years of his life. It couldn't just be the horror of prohibitions and medication, of things forgotten, of weariness, pain and routine. If that were the case, life would have defeated him, destroyed him without mercy, he, who had proclaimed that man can be destroyed but never defeated. Absolute rubbish: just rhetoric and lies, he thought, and poured himself another glass of wine. He needed to drink. That night threatened to be a bad one. But, if Miss Mary had been at home, perhaps it wouldn't have been the night that set in motion the end of his life.

They had hung a sign on the old wooden gate, dirty and faded, that warned CLOSED FOR STOCKTAKING. APOLOGIES FOR THE

INCONVENIENCE. Where the hell have they got that from? Conde wondered, also intrigued about the whereabouts of the original sign that Hemingway had decreed be put on that very same gate into Finca Vigía: UNINVITED GUESTS WILL NOT BE RECEIVED, just like that, uncompromising and in English, as if uninvited visitors could only reach that remote Cuban hideaway from the English-speaking world. And what about the rest of the world? What were they? Vermin? Conde pushed open one of the gates of the Finca, now turned into a museum, and he moved up towards the house long inhabited by the writer and then by his reputation, and through which had passed some of the most famous men and most beautiful women of the century.

No sooner had he set foot in that literary territory, first passing a mango tree and a couple of palm trees undoubtedly older than the house, than he felt as if he were returning to some sanctuary within his memory that he would have preferred to have kept hidden away, in the safe-keeping of a pleasant, contained nostalgia. He hadn't visited for more than twenty years – uninvited then, too – this place to which he had frequently gone on something like a solemn pilgrimage. The days were now far off when he merely dreamt of being a writer as well, and the whole myth of the old mountain leopard with his stock of stories of wars and hunting trips, with his short stories honed like knives and his novels full of life, with his dialogue that was simple yet at the same time complex, was his ideal model of what literature, and what a man with his life made by and for literature, should be like. In those days he had read all Hemingway's books, several times, and on many other occasions he had looked through the windows of the big house in Havana, which had been turned into a museum shortly after its owner's death, in order to seek out the spirit of the man amongst the hunting trophies he had won down the years.

Of all the trips undertaken to Hemingway's house in those nostalgia-haloed days, Conde remembered with particular pain the one that he had organised with his schoolfriends. He remembered it in minute detail: it had been a Saturday morning, and they had agreed to meet at the steps up to the school. Skinny Carlos, when he was still skinny; Dulcita, who was Skinny's girlfriend; Andrés, who was a good baseball player and who already dreamt of being a doctor, and didn't even imagine the possibility that he might one day leave Cuba; Rabbit, with his shiny Afro hairstyle and the wisdom that induced him to carry around two litres of rum in his rucksack; and Tamara, so beautiful that it hurt, and already the love of Mario Conde's life. His oldest and best friends were the apprentice writer's entourage on that pilgrimage and he could still derive pleasure from Tamara's amazement at the beauty of the place, from Andrés' joy at the view that you got of Havana from up in the tower of the house, from Rabbit's disgust at the number of hunting trophies hanging on the walls, and from the admiration of Red Candito on seeing that a single man could have so much house, just as he also remembered, with anguish and joy, the totally explicable disappearance of Carlos and Dulcita, who twenty minutes after breaking away from the group burst out from among the undergrowth happy and smiling, having just accomplished what was then their first mission in life: to have sex whenever the opportunity presented itself. It was a beautiful morning and Conde, overbearing and knowledgeable, a devoted admirer of the writer, seated his friends around the swimming pool and, passing around the bottles of rum, read them the whole of 'Big Two-Hearted River', his favourite of all Hemingway's short stories.

As he made his way up the path beneath the shade of the thick foliage of palms, ceiba trees, casuarinas and mangos, Conde tried to rid himself of that bitter-sweet recollection, and the certainty that time and life can destroy everything, but he only managed this when he finally made out the white structure of the house, and the tower that Mary Hemingway had had built for her husband to work in, and which ended up being the haunt of the fifty-seven cats who roamed the Finca. To his left, behind the hollow where the swimming pool was situated, he tried to catch the outline of the *Pilar*, removed from the water more than thirty years before and now also turned into a museum piece. The house, with all its doors and windows closed, without tourists or sightseers or trainee short-story writers peering into its preserved privacy, looked like a white ghost to Conde; something from the world of the dead. But he just looked at it for a moment, then carried on up the narrow tarmac path towards the higher part of the garden, from where there came the sound of voices and the irregular sound of a pickaxe and shovels single-minded in their probing of the earth.

The first thing he saw were the roots of the upturned mango tree. They were like the skeins of Medusa's hair, straggly and aggressive, appealing to the distant sky from where death had descended, and through which another death had been revealed. A bit further on in a pit already several metres long, he saw the heads of three men, above which were raised a pickaxe and shovels. Earth was flying towards a dark little heap that threatened to swallow up a fountain from which water had not issued for countless years. Conde walked over to the men in silence and recognised the owners of the shovels as two of his former police colleagues, Crespo and Greco, who were absorbed in an intense dialogue, while a man he didn't know was using the pickaxe.

'The last time I saw you, you were also in a hole.'

The men, surprised by his voice, turned round.

'My God,' said Greco. 'Well look who it is.'

The man with the pickaxe had also halted his work and was looking inquisitively at the newcomer.

'Don't tell me you're back,' said Crespo in amazement, as he struggled to climb out of the hole. For them the years had passed at the same speed as for Conde and they were now policemen in their forties with big bellies, who looked more suited, perhaps, to lying sunbathing on a beach.

'Not even I'm that crazy,' said Conde as he held out his hands to them to help them climb out.

'How long's it been, Conde?' Greco looked at him as if he were a museum piece.

'An age. Don't even try to work out how long.'

'Hell, it's great to see you. Manolo told us.'

'And who's that down in the hole?' asked Conde.

'Constable Fleites.'

'That old and he's still just a constable?'

'Take a good look at him, he's lame and short-sighted. And he writes poetry, but he gets pissed out of his mind, and just imagine . . .'

'At least he made it to constable,' said Conde as he waved to him. If he was as big a drunkard as they said, Constable Fleites was his kind of guy . . . 'And have you found anything yet?'

'There's no sign of anything down here, Conde,' protested Crespo.

'Don't tell me it was you who had the idea of opening up more holes?' Greco scolded him.

'Come on, don't get worked up down there: that was your boss's idea. I've got no authority around here . . .'

'Ah, so it was Manolito's idea . . . A bloody awful boss.'

'Come on, tell me the truth: who's the best boss, Manolo or me?'

Greco and Crespo looked at each other for a moment. They seemed to hesitate. It was Crespo who spoke:

'There's no contest, Conde: Manolo's an angel compared with you,' and they both laughed.

'You're a couple of ungrateful bastards . . .'

'Hey, Conde, since you're so clever and a bit of a writer . . .' Greco placed a dirty hand on his shoulder and looked scornfully towards Constable Fleites. 'Our colleague there says that one day Hemingway gave his wife a couple of kicks in the ass because she cut down a mango tree here at the Finca . . . is it true?'

'It wasn't a couple of kicks . . . it was three and a slap.'

From down in the hole Fleites smiled, glowing with pride.

'The guy was crazy,' confirmed Crespo.

'Yeah, a bit . . . but not that much: I read a book in which it says that to give your wife a couple of kicks in the ass is a perfectly healthy matrimonial action.'

'You don't need to read books to know that,' remarked Greco.

'So, nothing has turned up here?'

'After they removed all the bones, a bit of cloth

and what was left of his shoes, we've found nothing here but roots and stones.'

'But there must be something else. I've got a hunch. Look, I feel it here . . .' and Conde touched himself under his left nipple, pointing his fingers towards the painful source of the hunch. 'So carry on searching. Search until something turns up.'

'And what if nothing turns up?' Constable Fleites' voice reached them from the bottom of the hole.

'The Finca's large. Something'll turn up,' was Conde's reply. 'I'm going to see the director of the museum, I've got to get into the house . . . By the way, where did you find the notice you put on the gate?'

'From the pizzeria in the village. But it's just on loan,' warned Greco.

'Fine, I'll see you when you finish the hole,' and Conde started to move away.

'Hey, Conde,' Crespo shouted at him, 'you're really better off not being a cop.'

Conde smiled and went towards what had been the garage of the Finca, where the administrative office of the museum was now situated. The director, a man who was somewhat younger than Conde, introduced himself as Juan Tenorio. He was ugly, pleasant and tiresome, and the former cop at once tried to cut short his effusive verbal outpourings. Like a good director, Tenorio wanted to show off all that he knew about Hemingway and all that he knew about the Finca Vigía, and he volunteered to show Conde around. In the clearest and nicest way possible, Conde turned down the offer. His first visit inside the house was something between Hemingway and himself, and he needed to do it quietly, without witnesses.

'It's ten o'clock . . . how long can I stay in there?' Conde asked him, after getting the keys of the house.

'Well, we finish at four o'clock. But if you . . .'

'No, I'll leave at four. But I need to be left undisturbed. Thanks.'

And he turned his back on the director of the museum.

Conde went up the six steps that separated the drive from the embankment on which the house was built and took a deep breath. He went up the remaining six steps that led to the front door, put the key in the lock and opened the door. As he stepped inside the house, he felt he was committing himself irretrievably to Hemingway's mystery.

He stretched out a hand and found a switch. He put on the light in the drawing-room. Before his eyes the panorama of what had once been a home in which people had lived, slept, eaten, loved and suffered, opened up, dimly frozen in time. But it wasn't just the signs that the place had been converted into a museum that gave it such a highly unreal feeling: the Vigía house had always been a kind of stage, a backdrop, made to fit the character more than the man. Conde found it all highly offensive – the thousands of books and tens of paintings and drawings placed in bitter competition with rifles, bullets, spears and knives, and the motionless, accusing heads of some of the victims of Hemingway's acts of manliness, his hunting trophies, collected simply for the pleasure of killing, for the contrived sensation of living dangerously.

Many other pictures were now missing from

the house, having been removed from Cuba by Mary Welsh; missing too were some papers and letters that it was felt certain his widow had burnt on her last trip back to the Finca, just after the author's death. Missing also were the people who would have been able to give the place life: the owners, the servants, the regular visitors and the special guests, as well as the occasional journalist able to overcome the 'uninvited' barrier to have a few minutes' conversation with the living god of North American literature. But above all, there was a lack of natural light. Conde went through the house opening up the shutters one by one, starting in the drawing-room and ending in the kitchen and bathrooms. The warming glow of the morning light cheered the place up; the smell of flowers and earth flooded into the house and Conde gradually began to wonder what it was he was looking for. He knew that it was not clues to the identity of the dead man whose body had appeared in the yard, still less physical proof of who was responsible for the murder. He was searching for something further off, something that he had already pursued on one occasion and which, a few years back, he had stopped searching for: the truth – or perhaps the true lie – about Ernest Miller Hemingway.

In order to start that difficult process, Conde committed the ultimate act of sacrilege: he took off his own shoes and put on the writer's old moccasins, which were several sizes too big for him. He went back to the drawing-room, dragging his feet, lit a cigarette and settled himself into the personal armchair of the man who wanted people to call him 'Papa'. As he sat there, revelling in his disrespectful behaviour, Conde examined the oil paintings of bullfights and, without consciously setting out to do so, remembered how his reverence for the writer had come to an end when he discovered certain facts about the end of the old friendship between Hemingway and his former colleague, John Dos Passos. In fact he had not suddenly stopped loving Hemingway when he came across that information; his alienation had grown as his literary idol had been revealed as an arrogant and violent person, unable to give love to those who loved him; when Conde realised that more than twenty years living alongside Cubans were not enough for the artist to understand a damned thing about their island; when he finally accepted the painful truth that this genius of a writer was also a contemptible man, capable of betraying each of those who helped him, from Sherwood Anderson to 'poor' Scott Fitzgerald. The final straw was when he found out about the cruel, sadistic way in which he had treated Dos Passos during the years of the Spanish Civil War. Dos Passos had insisted on investigating the truth about the death of his Spanish friend José Robles, while Hemingway, in the middle of a public meeting, crowed that Robles had been shot as a spy and traitor to the Republican cause. Then, exceeding all the bounds of friendship, he had cruelly made Robles the model for the traitor in *For Whom the Bell Tolls* . . . The end of the friendship between the two writers and the start of Dos Passos's political reconversion began when Dos Passos found out that Robles, too close to some unsavoury goings-on, had actually been one of the first victims of the Stalinist terror unleashed in Spain in 1936 (when those pathetic trials were being held in Moscow). Stalin had wanted to ensure Soviet influence in the Republican side, but shortly afterwards he had betrayed them, and left them in the hands of the Fascists. Out of that shady, deplorable story, expanded by Hemingway, Dos Passos had emerged as a coward and he as a hero. The truth, however, would eventually be known, and with it spread the extent to which Hemingway and his credulous vanity were instruments in the hands of the Stalinist propaganda machine of those terrible times. Conde felt a bitter taste in his mouth every time he remembered that dark episode, and now, in the midst of so many things bought, hunted and given to their owner, a man whose envy had seemed capable of destroying all the writers in the world, he concluded that he would be happy to find a trail leading him to Hemingway's guilt: it would suit him quite well if he turned out to be a common murderer.

It had rained all afternoon. With the windows now closed and the light turned off, Conde felt under siege from hunger and the soft summer heat, and

lay down on the bed in Mary Welsh's room to wait
for the rain to stop. How often will love have been
made in this bed? How often will some of the
employees of the museum have desecrated it in the
course of their extra-marital adventures? His search
of the place had lasted barely three hours, but it
was enough to convince him that he needed to know
a lot more about the story behind those bones if
he wanted anything he found at the house to speak
clearly to him in some revealing way. He had,
however, already confirmed three of his suspicions.
The first was foreseeable: in this house there were
some books that would probably achieve high prices
in the Havana markets for which he worked.
Secondly, that there must have been something of
the masochist in Hemingway if the rumour that he
used to write standing up, with the portable Royal
typewriter on a bookcase, were true, since writing,
as Conde knew only too well, is sufficiently difficult
in itself without being made into a physical as well
as a mental challenge. And finally, on top of all that,
Hemingway had added an element of sadism to his
masochism, since all those stuffed heads spread over

the walls of the house indicated too great a taste for pointlessly spilt blood and violence for its own sake for one not to feel a certain repulsion towards the author of so much death.

It was after four when he was woken by knocking on the door and, like a sleepwalker, Conde went to the drawing-room and ran into the nervous face of the museum's director.

'I thought something had happened to you.'

'No, I just got tired.'

'Did you find anything?'

'I don't know yet. Has it stopped raining?'

'It's stopping now.'

'And what about the police?'

'They left when it started to rain. Their excavation's turned into a lake.'

'You going into Havana?'

'Yes, as far as Santos Suárez.'

'Will you give me a lift?' ventured Conde.

Just as he'd feared, Tenorio spoke the whole time: he really did know Hemingway's Cuban life like the back of his hand and was a resolute admirer of the writer. Well, since he owes his living to him, that's just as well, thought Conde, and he let him talk while he mulled over the information in his brain, which still felt dulled by sleep.

'We Cuban Hemingwayians are anxious that all this should be sorted out. I for one am certain that it wasn't him . . .'

'You Cuban Hemingwayians? What's that, a Masonic lodge or a political party?'

'Neither: we're people who like Hemingway. And we're from all walks of life: writers, journalists, teachers, housewives and retired people.'

'And what do you Cuban Hemingwayians do?'

'Well nothing much, we read Hemingway, study him, have conferences about his life.'

'And who runs that?'

'Nobody . . . well, I organise people a bit, but nobody runs it.'

'It's faith for its own sake, but without a church or priests. That's not a bad idea,' admitted Conde, full of admiration at the existence of a brotherhood of independent believers at a time of unionised unbelievers.

'No, it's not faith. The fact is that he was a

great writer and not the ogre he is sometimes portrayed as. And aren't you a Hemingwayian?'

Conde had to think for a moment before replying.

'I was, but I handed back my membership card.'

'Are you a cop or aren't you a cop?'

'No, I'm not. That's to say, I'm not a cop any longer either.'

'Then what are you? That's if you don't mind telling me.'

'I wish I knew . . . Right now I'm sure about what I don't want to be. And one of the things that I don't want to be is a cop: I've seen too many people turning into bastards when their job should be making life fucking difficult for real bastards.'

'That's true,' admitted Tenorio after he'd given the matter some thought.

'And, as a convinced Hemingwayian, what do you think about this story?'

'What happened to that dead man is a mystery. But I'm certain that Hemingway didn't kill him. I know because I've spoken a lot with the old men who knew him — with Raúl Villaroy when he was alive, with Ruperto, the skipper of the *Pilar*, and also with Toribio Hernández, the person who was in charge of Hemingway's fighting cocks . . .'

'Toribio el Tuzao? Is he still alive?' Conde said in amazement. According to his calculations and his memory the man must be about two hundred years old, perhaps more.

'Alive and saying terrible things about Hemingway, although he's not always truthful and says whatever he feels like at the time . . . Well, talking to those people I realised that Hemingway was a better person than he seemed. He had done each of these people a good turn in life. And I include here many of his friends. He had done all of his employees very specific favours: he had forgiven some for serious things and allowed them to carry on working in the Finca, he helped others out of difficult situations. And he used to pay them very well. That's why almost every one of those who worked with him would even kill for Papa if he asked.'

'Even kill for him?'

'That's just an expression . . .' the director realised that he had perhaps gone too far, but he remained insistent on this point. 'Yes, I believe that some of them were capable of killing.'

'That sounds like the Godfather. I do you a favour and then you're in my debt. It's a way of buying people.'

'No, it wasn't like that.'

'Well, persuade me . . .'

'Raúl Villaroy. When Hemingway came to live in the Vigía, Raúl was a raggle-taggle orphan dying of hunger. Hemingway virtually adopted him. He changed his life, he made him into a person, and naturally Raúl used to see things through the eyes of his boss. Although he wasn't the only one. Ruperto still worships him, just like the Galician, Ferrer, the one who was his doctor. And Toribio himself, despite all that he says, would have done anything Hemingway asked of him. Well then, what did you think of the inside of the house?'

Conde looked at the street, still wet from the recent rain, and he tried to take in the way in which Hemingway had been able to manipulate gratitude. That relationship of dependency could be the beginning of a dangerous conspiracy.

'Had you been in there before?' insisted Tenorio, refusing to leave without the reply he wanted.

'No. It was all very interesting,' said Conde in an attempt to end the conversation.

'But you didn't see the weapons.'

'No. They're in the tower, aren't they?'

'Yes. And I bet you didn't see Ava Gardner's knickers either.'

Conde felt a pang.

'Whose knickers?'

'Ava Gardner's.'

'You sure about them?'

'Couldn't be surer.'

'No, I didn't see them. But I've got to see them. The nearest thing to seeing a woman naked is seeing her underwear. I must see them. What colour are they?'

'Black, with lace. Hemingway used them to wrap around his .22 revolver.'

'I must see them,' repeated Conde, like one of Hemingway's characters, and, after thanking him for all his help, asked Tenorio to leave him on the next corner, without plucking up the courage to ask him which of his parents had committed the nominal sin of lumbering him for life with that resonant and Don Juanesque name.

Conde enjoyed walking through Havana on summer evenings after heavy rainfall. The overwhelming heat would withdraw until the next day and there remained in the air a damp taste that he found comforting, like rum, and which gave him the strength to face up to the great sorrows in his life.

Skinny Carlos was in the doorway of his house. Although he hadn't been skinny for many years now, but a fat mass stuck in a wheelchair, Conde insisted upon calling him by the nickname that he'd given him in the old days at school, when Carlos was very skinny and nobody thought that one day he would come back an invalid from someone else's war. They had shared an honest, true friendship for so long now that they were more than friends, and every night Conde visited him so they could listen to the same music that they had been listening to for twenty years, speak about whatever they wanted, drink whatever there was to drink and wolf down, voraciously, the amazing dishes prepared by Josefina, Carlos' mother.

'Didn't you get caught in the rain, you old bastard?' Skinny asked him as he saw him come in.

'I got caught by something far worse: a pair of knickers,' and Conde told him the story of the black knickers, covered in lace and the memory of Ava Gardner's skin, which he hadn't seen in Hemingway's house, although he couldn't think of anything else now.

'You're losing your touch,' concluded Carlos, 'for you to miss a pair of knickers like that . . .'

'It's because I'm not a cop any more,' replied Conde defensively.

'Don't give me that shit, you don't need to be a cop to find a pair of Ava Gardner's knickers.'

'But it helps, doesn't it?'

'Of course. But you're a private detective now. Sounds strange, doesn't it?'

'Damn strange,' pondered Conde, trying to come to terms with his new status. 'So I'm a private dick now. How about that, eh?'

'And what else didn't you discover, Marlowe?'

'Loads of things, Skinny. I didn't discover who killed the dead man, nor who the hell the corpse could have been. But I did discover something sad, lonely and final: the person I want the murderer to be.'

'The whole of Havana knows that, Conde . . . The incredible thing is that you should have liked him so much before.'

'I liked the way he wrote.'

'Who are you kidding? You liked the guy as well. You used to say that he was a legend. Remember the day you forced us all to go to the Finca?'

'It seems incredible, but I was certain he was a legend. And yet, he still has some redeeming features: he couldn't bear politicians and he liked dogs.'

'He preferred cats.'

'Really? Bah, he must have been . . .'

'By the way, have you had any more news from Tamara?'

Conde looked out towards the street. Two months ago Tamara had set out on a trip to Milan, where her twin sister lived, and communications from her had become less and less frequent. Although Conde had avoided formalising any relationship with the woman he liked as much at forty-five as he had done at eighteen, and whose absence forced upon him an irksome chastity, the mere idea that Tamara might not come back gave him pains in his stomach, in his heart, and in other worse places . . .

'Don't talk to me about that,' he said, in a quieter voice.

'She'll come back, Conde.'

'Yes, if you say so . . .'

'You're hurting badly, old friend.'

'I'm suffering.'

Carlos shook his head. He was sorry that he had brought up this topic and looked for an easy way of changing the subject.

'I was just reading your Hemingway-style short stories. They're pretty good, Conde.'

'You've still got those papers stashed away? You told me you were going to chuck them out . . .'

'But I didn't chuck them out and I'm not going to give them to you.'

'That's just as well. Because if I get my hands on them, I'll rip them up. I'm more and more certain that Hemingway was a bad guy. To start with, he didn't have any friends . . .'

'That's serious.'

'Extremely serious, Skinny. As serious as the hunger I'm suffering from right now. Can you inform me of the whereabouts of the Magician of the Cooking-pot?'

'She went out to get extra virgin olive oil for the salad . . .'

'Let me have it,' demanded Conde.

'Well it's like this, the Old Lady told me that food's in short supply today. I think that she's only going to make a *quimbombo* stew with pork and ham, white rice, fried *malanga*, avocado salad, watercress and tomato, and for dessert *guayaba* jam with white cheese . . . yes and she's also going to warm up some ground maize *tamales* left over from yesterday.'

'How many *tamales* survived?'

'We left about ten. There were more than forty, weren't there?'

'Ten. We're losing our touch. In the past we

would have downed the lot, wouldn't we? The worst of it is that I haven't got a cent to buy some rum with, and I'm desperate for a drink . . .'

Skinny Carlos smiled. Conde liked seeing him smile: it was one of the few things he still liked in life. The world was disintegrating, people were changing sides as it happened, and his own country seemed more and more alien and unfamiliar to him, but despite the sorrows and losses, Skinny Carlos preserved intact his capacity to smile, even to reassure.

'But you and I aren't like Hemingway and we do have friends . . . Good friends. Go to my room and grab the litre bottle that's next to the tape recorder. Know who gave me it? Red Candito. Since he doesn't drink now he brought me the bottle he got on his ration book: a Santa Cruz rum, that is.'

Skinny stopped talking as it was obvious that his friend was no longer listening to him. He'd gone into the house like a bandit and was emerging from it with a piece of bread between his teeth, two glasses in one hand and the bottle of rum in the other.

'Know what I've just discovered?' he said, the bread still between his teeth.

'No, what?' asked Skinny as he took his glass.

'In the bathroom window there's a pair of knickers belonging to old Josie . . . And to think that I didn't even notice Ava Gardner's!'

He looked at the Chianti bottle with loathing: he'd finished the wine and his glass was empty. He slowly placed the glass and the bottle on the floor and stretched back once more in his chair. He felt the temptation to look at his watch, but he restrained himself. Without looking at the time he took it off his wrist and dropped it between the glass and the bottle, on the soft oriental carpet. For that one night there would no more rules or restrictions. He'd do some of the things he enjoyed and, to start with, he began to enjoy the enervating pleasure of scratching his nose with his fingernail to remove those white flakes of skin that disgusted Miss Mary. It's a benign cancer, he used to say, as he had suffered from patches of melanoma since the days when he used to spend too long exposed to the sun in the Tropics, while he was leading the expedition in the *Pilar* hunting for Nazi submarines.

In fact, what really horrified his wife – and he knew it – was to see him carrying out this operation in public, sometimes at the meal table. Miss Mary had struggled to teach him good manners and decent habits. She tried to ensure that he didn't wear dirty clothes, that he bathed every day and that he wore underpants (at least if he was going out into the street), and she endeavoured to dissuade him from combing his hair in front of people to avoid the spectacle of his plentiful dandruff, and from shouting out insults in the language of the Ojibwa Indians of Michigan. And she made a special request to him not to scratch his flaky skin. But all her efforts had been fruitless, since he insisted on appearing shocking and aggressive, so as to raise a further barrier between himself and the rest of humankind, although the question of his peeling skin had nothing to do with his old poses: it was the call of a pleasure welling up from his subconscious and for that reason it could catch him unawares absolutely anywhere.

He had almost three hundred scars on his body – more than two hundred of them received in a single incident, when he was hit by a hand grenade at Fossalta as he was transporting a wounded soldier on his back – and he could tell a good story about each of them, though he was no longer sure of their veracity. For instance his head, the last time that he shaved it, resembled a map of a world full of fury and heat, wrecked by earthquakes and embedded with volcanoes. Of all the wounds that he would most have liked to exhibit, however, there was only one that had eluded him: the goring of a bull, something that he had been very near to achieving on two occasions.

He regretted having allowed his thoughts to wander in this direction, since if there was something that he did not want to remember it was bullfighting, along with his work and his wretched revision of *Death in the Afternoon*, which refused to flow along easy channels. It all provoked in him an unhealthy longing for those days long past, when things went so well in his writing that he could recreate the countryside and stroll through it, and walking among trees emerge into woodland clearings, and go up a hill until he could make out the downlands beyond the shore of the lake. Then, he would have been able almost to put his arm through the shoulder strap of his rucksack, wet with sweat, and lift it up and put his other arm through the other strap, spreading the weight over his back, and literally feel the pine needles beneath his moccasins as he started to walk down the slope towards the lake . . .

With a feeling of anguish pressing upon his chest he decided that it was time to set out. It must have been after eleven o'clock and the wine's liberating effect was making its presence felt in its treacherous capacity for evocation. He stood up and opened the door. On the rug in the entrance hall Black Dog was waiting for him, as loyal as a dog should be.

'They tell me you haven't eaten and I can't believe it,' he addressed the animal, which was now wagging its tail. Since the day more than thirteen years before when he had picked him up as a puppy in a street in Cojímar, this dog, whose tangled hair was now shot through with grey, had struck up a loving relationship of dependence with his master, who had singled him out from among the other dogs at the Finca. 'Come on, let's put that right.'

Black Dog seemed doubtful about the invitation. Miss Mary didn't let the dogs into the house, though some of the cats were permitted.

'Come on in, that crazy woman's away . . .'

And he clicked his fingers for the animal to follow him. Timidly at first, but then more confidently, the dog followed him through to the kitchen. Armed with a knife, Hemingway began to slice the *jamón serrano* resting in its rack. He knew that Black Dog could turn down anything but *jamón serrano*. He threw several scraps into the air. The dog caught them one by one and swallowed them almost without chewing them.

'Well, well, old Black Dog can still catch things in mid-flight. That means he's better, doesn't it? We're going straight out.'

He went to the bathroom adjoining his

bedroom and opened his flies. It took some time for the stream of urine to flow, and when it did, it was like expelling hot sand. Briefly shaking dry his limp member, he put it away and walked over to his desk. From the top drawer, in which he also kept invoices and cheques, he took the .22 calibre revolver that always accompanied him on his rounds of the Finca. He had chosen a pair of black knickers that Ava Gardner had left at the house to wrap the weapon. The knickers and the revolver, together, served to remind him that there had been better times, when he pissed with a powerful, crystal-clear stream. He picked up his three-battery torch from the floor and checked that it worked. Just as he was about to leave his room some premonition made him go back, and he took from the shelf where he kept his hunting weapons his Thompson machine gun, which had been with him since 1935 and with which he had once killed sharks. Three days previously he had cleaned it and he had forgotten, as always, to put it back where it was usually stored, on the second floor of the tower. The weapon was the same model as that used by Harry Morgan in *To Have and Have Not*, and by Eddy, Thomas Hudson's friend and cook, in *Islands in the Stream*. He stroked the short butt, felt the pleasant coldness of the barrel and placed a full clip in it, as if he were going off to war.

Black Dog was waiting for him in the drawing-room. The animal greeted him with barks of joy, urging him to hurry up. His greatest pleasure was feeling himself near to his master on those patrols from which the other two dogs of the Finca, and of course the cats, were excluded. 'You're a great dog,' Hemingway told him, 'a great and good dog.'

He went out through the side door of the drawing-room, which opened out onto the terrace and led to the Portuguese-tiled water-tank made by the Finca's original owner. As he went towards the path that led to the swimming pool, he enjoyed the feeling of being armed and protected. It was a long time since he had fired the Thompson; perhaps the last time had been when he went out into the Gulf in search of a giant marlin with the producers of the film of *The Old Man and The Sea*. And now he wasn't sure why he had decided to take it with him on his innocuous patrol that night, not imagining that for the rest of his life he would repeat that question to himself until it became a painful obsession. Perhaps he took it because he had been thinking about it for days and had continually postponed its return to the weapons store; perhaps because it was the preferred weapon of Gregory, the most pigheaded of his sons, from whom he had hardly heard anything since the death of his mother, the good-natured Pauline; or perhaps it was because, ever since he was a child, he had felt a passionate attraction towards firearms. This attraction began to emerge at the age of ten, when his grandfather Hemingway had made him a present of a small, single-barrel, twelve-bore shotgun which he would always remember as the best present he had ever received. Shooting and killing became from that moment one of his favourite occupations, something that was almost necessary to him, despite his father's maxim that one should only kill to eat. Naturally, he very soon forgot that rule, the dramatic nature of which he must have understood once, at least on the day his father forced him to eat the tough flesh of the porcupine at which he had taken a pot-shot just for the pleasure of shooting.

Firearms and their role in killing became for him, little by little, one of the literary definitions of manliness and bravery: that's why all his great heroes had carried firearms and used them, sometimes on other people. He, however, who had killed thousands of birds, hordes of sharks and marlins, and even rhinos, gazelles, impalas, buffaloes, lions and zebras, had never killed a man, despite having been in three wars and many other skirmishes. It backfired on him badly when he put about the story that he himself had thrown a hand grenade into a cellar in which were hidden some members of the Gestapo who were preventing the advance of his band of guerrillas upon Paris. He had had to deny what he himself had said before a court martial, to which he had been brought by the other war correspondents, who accused him of having participated in military actions under the cover of journalism. Why hadn't he maintained his lie if there was hardly any risk of him losing a credential which, in actual fact, meant so little to him? Why had he testified in his defence if the only thing harmed by his testimony was his own myth as a man of action? But, above all, why hadn't he thrown the grenade and killed those men? He still didn't know why, and not knowing bothered him.

The heavy rain that afternoon had freshened up the trees and the grass. The air was damp but comfortable and, before going down to the main gate where Calixto was on duty, he made his way to the swimming pool and walked around it. He paused in front of the graves of Black Dog's predecessors and tried to remember something of the character of each of them. They had all been good dogs, especially Nero, but none of them had been like Black Dog.

'You're the best dog I've ever had,' he said to the animal, who had walked over on seeing him bending over the little heaps of earth, crowned by the small wooden boards that identified them.

He refused to think any more about death and carried on with his walk. He was walking round the flower-decked pergola, where the changing-rooms were, when a dry leaf fell from a tree and landed with brief ripples on the surface of the dead water. That slight break in an always fragile balance was enough to cause the fresh and shining image of Adriana Ivancich, swimming in the moonlight, to burst from the water. He had found it tough to convince himself of the need to stay away from that young woman, from whom he knew he could only expect fleeting pleasure and long suffering: and although it wasn't the first time he had fallen in love with the wrong person, the evidence that his mistake was related solely to her age and talents was the first serious warning of the aggressive approach of old age. If he could no longer love, or hunt, or drink, or fight, and almost not write, what was the purpose of living? He stroked the shining barrel of the Thompson and looked towards the silent world spread out at his feet. And on the other side of the pergola, shining on the tiles, he saw it.

When he understood that it was neither an air-raid nor the arrival of a hurricane, he realised that this was his second turbulent awakening in two days.

'Hey, Conde, I can't spend all morning on this,' shouted the aggressive voice, while the hands continued to knock on the wooden door.

He had to think about it three times, and attempt it three more times, before he finally managed to get to his feet. His knee, his neck and his waist hurt him. What's *not* hurting you, Mario Conde? he asked himself. My head, he replied to himself, gratefully, after the mental examination to which he submitted his poor anatomy. His brain, strangely functional, allowed him to remember that the previous night, when they were playing the requiem for the bottle of Santa Cruz, Rabbit had arrived with a litre of homemade spirit manufactured and sold by Pedro the Viking, which they had polished off while devouring the *tamales* left for the end of the meal. They listened to the music of Credence and, at Carlos' insistence, they even read one of Conde's old Hemingway stories – the story of a settling of scores which, suddenly, became a new settling of scores between Conde and his oldest and most remote literary hero-worship. But his alcoholic tolerance now couldn't be what it once was. Ah, what the hell, he said to himself as he picked his way between the boxes of books from the last batch he had acquired, remembering other far from calm mornings which had followed nights that had been much more riotous and boozy. So when he opened the door he warned:

'Keep quiet for five minutes. Let me have a piss and make some coffee.'

Inspector Palacios, used to receiving this kind of treatment, kept quiet. With an unlit cigarette between his fingers he observed with interest the boxes of books scattered around the house, and went through to the kitchen. Conde came out of the bathroom and prepared the coffee. Without a word, without looking at one another, the men waited for the coffee to be ready. Conde served two cups, a large one for him, another smaller one for Manolo. He began to sip the hot drink: each sip that passed through his mouth slipped down his throat and fell into his distant stomach, rousing one of his few surviving neurones. Eventually he lit a cigarette and looked at his former colleague.

'Did you see Garbage outside the door?'

'Not exactly outside the door,' said Manolo. 'He was hanging out over at the street corner with a gang of dogs, chasing a bitch.'

'I haven't set eyes on that bastard for three days now. I've got the kind of dog I deserve: crazy and horny.'

'Can I say something now?'

'Go ahead. Get it all off your chest . . .'

'Forget the Hemingway story and carry on selling books. What I've got for you now is a bomb. A real bomb.'

'What's happened?'

'Yesterday's downpour helped Crespo and Greco. It brought this out of the earth.'

He dropped a nylon bag with a metal identity badge in it onto the table. The badge had remnants of black leather sticking to it. On the rusty surface of the metal it was possible to make out some lines that traced the shape of a shield, some corroded and unrecognisable numbers and three alarming letters: FBI.

'Well, fuck me!' Conde had to concede.

Inspector Palacios smiled with satisfaction.

'The guy knocked off a federal agent.'

'This doesn't prove anything . . .' Conde pointed to the badge, without much enthusiasm.

'What do you mean? Look, this makes clear that his delusion that the FBI were after him was for real. It's been known for years that they were after him and this really puts the lid on it, Conde. A real bomb, isn't it?'

Mario Conde stubbed out his cigarette and took hold of the envelope with the badge inside it. 'This explains a lot of things, but not everything.'

'I know, I know. We have to find out if an FBI agent disappeared in Cuba between '57 and '60. And, if possible, discover what he was doing here.'

'Keeping an eye on Hemingway? Blackmailing him?'

'Could be. And if it's true . . .'

'And what if it wasn't him who did the killing, Manolo?'

'Well, he can get stuffed. But with all that evidence, the prize is his. He's going to be up to his ears in shit . . .'

Conde got up. He turned on the tap, washed his face and dampened his hair. He dried around his eyes and mouth with the threadbare pullover in which he had slept. He poured out what was left of the coffee and lit another cigarette, reflecting that the clearest proof that his alcoholic tolerance had diminished was when he'd experienced, as he'd read Skinny and Rabbit his old Hemingway-styled story, a vague and disconcerting feeling that had caused his prejudices against the master, whom he had so much admired and hated, to waver.

'Let me tell you something, Manolo . . . I don't want to rush to any conclusions, although you know I would be delighted if it were him. But you've got to have balls to kill a man, and I'm not sure that he had sufficient balls to do it.'

'Steady on, Conde! What did you have to drink yesterday?'

'Don't start on at me about that . . . I'm not certain it was him and that's all there is to it. I've got an idea: hold onto the badge for three days. Give me three days.'

'Now you've gone crazy. Listen, everybody knows that Hemingway had an arsenal of firearms in his house, and I checked with the director of the museum, who confirmed that he went around the Finca carrying a pistol with him the whole time . . . If you meet a guy wandering around your house one night and you're carrying a pistol . . . It's not a matter of balls. Listen, why don't you just drop this affair and get on with selling books and writing – and let's see if you can wrap up one of your books and become a real writer.'

Conde stood up and looked out through the window. The weather outside was beautiful and it was already hot.

'So I should become a real writer. I'm a pretend one now, am I?'

'Don't be so touchy, you know what I mean.'

'And you also know what I mean. You still haven't found the bullets. You don't know what they killed that federal agent with.'

'We don't need to any more.'

Conde felt a strange unease. All his prejudices and his desire to prove Hemingway's guilt had fallen into the lake of his memory and he now watched them sinking dramatically, in the face of his disconcerting realisation that his hatred was not as strong as his archaic sense of justice.

'And don't forget that he used to spend months at a time away from the Finca. Probably on one of those occasions . . .'

'What the hell's wrong with you? So you've gone all soft? To start with, I'm not going to say that he killed him: merely that the dead man turned up in his house, and next to the body, this . . .' and he placed a hand over the badge.

'Forget you're a cop for a moment, Manolo. They're going to pounce on you like vultures. They're going to turn this story into a political issue. That's what pisses me off most about it.'

'It was all of his own making, wasn't it? Didn't he play at being a guerrilla fighter and defending the Communists? It was very easy the way he did it: a guerrilla with water bottles full of whisky and gin hanging from his belt, a

Communist with a yacht and enough money to live as he chose. Ah, Conde, I've had it with those bastards who live like princes and talk of justice and equality.'

'Listen, Manolo,' Conde went back to his seat and picked up the envelope containing the badge, 'everything you say is true and you know I'm on your side in this. But if that dead man has been missing for forty years, no harm will be done if you put this badge away for three days. Keep the museum closed and let me investigate. Do this for me, not for him . . . it's a favour I'm asking.'

'You're asking me for favours? Now we're fucked. Don't tell me you've got a hunch.'

Conde smiled, for the first time that day.

'I haven't even got that. What I've got is something I owe myself. I worshipped that man and now I can't stand him. But the fact is I don't know him. What's more, I don't think anyone knows him. Let me find out who he was: that's what I want to do. Then I'll probably be able to tell what happened.'

'But I've got to say something, my bosses . . .'

'You'll think of something, just like I taught you.'

'You're going to land me in it, Mario Conde.'

'No . . . you'll see, it'll be alright. Put away the badge and give me three days. And in the meantime, there's something for you to do: read "Big Two-Hearted River" and tell me what you think of it.'

'I've already read it, ages ago . . . at your insistence.'

'Read it again. Do it for me.'

'OK, I'll read it, but I don't understand why the hell you want to get to understand a man who, from what you yourself say, nobody knew . . .'

Conde yawned and looked at his former colleague.

'I don't know, I honestly don't know . . . That's just the way we real writers are, right?'

It might have been the last of the mummies. A skilful embalmer of pharaohs had worked the miracle of placing it upright in a chair and, with Egyptian patience, had arranged each one of the folds in its skin until it had succeeded in making it look as much alive as dead. Conde looked at him for a few moments. He focused his attention on the work of art achieved with the hands, on which the scars, the stretch marks on the skin, the veins and wrinkles all formed an amazing network. He finally plucked up the courage to touch him. Slowly, the old man's eyelids folded back, like those of a sleepy reptile, and eyes of a faded blue recoiled at the aggressive light.

'What's the matter?' he spoke, and Conde was surprised: his voice was not that of an old man.

'I wanted to talk to you, Toribio.'

'Who are you?'

'You don't know me, but you were a friend of my grandfather, Rufino Conde.'

The old man made an effort to smile.

'That guy was dangerous . . . a real cheat . . .'

'Yes, I know. I used to help him with his fighting cocks.'

'Rufino's dead, isn't he?'

'Yes, years ago. After they banned cock-fights. They were his life.'

'And mine. It fucking goes to show, they banned cockfights years ago and everyone's dead. I don't fucking know why I'm still alive. I can hardly see now.'

'How old are you, Toribio?'

'One hundred and two years, three months and eighteen days . . .'

Conde smiled. At times he forgot his own age. But he understood that every day that passed must be important for Toribio el Tuzao, because he was getting nearer and nearer to the end of his allotted time. In Conde's remotest memories there was the figure of Toribio, already ancient, as he checked over a fighting cock: he examined its spurs, stretched out its wings, made sure of the strength of the muscles in its legs, examined its claws, opened its beak, felt its neck, and then lovingly stroked the animal destined for combat and death. His grandfather Rufino, who rarely bestowed any praise on his opponents, maintained that Tuzao was one of the best breeders of fighting cocks in Cuba. Perhaps for that reason Hemingway had taken him on and made him, for years, the sole trainer of his birds.

'And how many years did you work for Hemingway?'

'Twenty-one, until he died. And then I inherited his fighting cocks. They were worth a fortune. He made a present of them to me. Papa wrote that in his last will and testament.'

'Was Papa a good guy?'

'A real bastard, but he liked fighting cocks. He needed me, you know.'

'Why was he a real bastard?'

Toribio el Tuzao didn't reply at once. He seemed to be weighing up his words. Conde tried to imagine the workings of his pre-computer age, nineteenth-century brain, around since before the invention of the cinema, aeroplanes and the ball-point pen.

'One day he lost his temper and tore the head off a cockerel that had backed down in a training fight in the little ring we had in the Vigía. I couldn't stand for that and we came to blows. I hit him and he hit me. I told him that he could stick his cockerels up his ass and that he was a criminal, that you didn't treat a fighting cock like that.'

'But if they kill each other fighting, they gouge each others' eyes out . . . many trainers put them down if they lose their sight.'

'That's another matter: the fight is the fight, and it's between cocks. And it's not the same, putting down an animal so that it won't suffer, as killing it in a fit of anger.'

'That's true. And what happened afterwards?'

'He wrote me a letter apologising. He was such an idiot that he forgot that I couldn't read. I forgave him and he hired a teacher who taught me how to read. But this didn't make him any the less of a real bastard.'

Conde smiled and lit a cigarette.

'Why did they call you Tuzao – "the plucked one"?'

'Some cock trainers gave me the nickname when I was a boy. One day when they shaved my head with one of those machines used to shear horses that leaves your hair very short and spiky, one of them said to me: Look, you're like a shorn cockerel. And that's what they've called me ever since . . . I've spent all my life involved in cockfights.'

'My grandfather Rufino thought highly of you as a cock trainer.'

'Rufino was one of the good ones. Although he was too much of a cheat. He didn't like losing.'

'He used to say that in order to gamble, you had to start with an advantage.'

'That's why he never fought against my cocks. I knew what he did to his animals. He used to put Vaseline on his neck, and while they bathed and weighed the cocks your grandfather would rub the back of his neck with his hand, as if it were hurting him, and then when he took hold of the cockerel, he left it like a bar of soap . . . a fucking crafty devil.'

Conde smiled again. He enjoyed hearing those stories about his grandfather. They cast him back to a lost world which in the free territory of his memory greatly resembled happiness.

'Did Hemingway know anything about cock-fighting?'

'Of course he knew something . . . I taught him,' Toribio assured him and tried to settle his skeleton into the chair. 'If you want proof of this, when he left Cuba to kill himself he told me that as soon as he had finished the book about bullfighters he was going to write one about cock breeders.'

'It would've been a great book.'

'Of course it would've been a great book,' the old man stated emphatically.

'And did he bet heavily?'

'Yes, heavily, he was a born gambler. On horses, on cockerels . . . and the bastard was lucky, he almost always won. But after winning, he used to get drunk, and at times he would spend the money and give away all his winnings. Money wasn't important to him; what he liked was the fight. He was obsessed with fights and with the courage of the cocks. He loved seeing a cock lose its sight with two blows from its opponent's spurs and then carry on fighting without being able to see its adversary. That really excited him.'

'He was a strange guy, wasn't he?

'A real bastard, I told you. My theory is he had a demon in him. That's why he drank so much – to appease the demon.'

'That's for sure . . . And did you live at the Finca?'

'No, none of those who worked with him lived at the Finca. Not even Raúl, who was always with him and was like Papa's shadow. Let's see: except for Ruperto and me, they were all from around there, from San Francisco. And Raúl lived very close, almost at the entrance to the Finca.'

'And at night did he used to stay alone in the house?'

'Well, not alone, with his wife. And there were almost always guests staying there. But, in the end, when Papa was old, she sometimes told Calixto to stay as a watchman at the lower gate or in the bungalow next to the garages.'

'A watchman? I thought he did a patrol around the Finca himself before going to bed.'

'That's if he wasn't too drunk to manage it. But Miss Mary was happier if the watchman was there . . .'

This didn't fit Conde's theory: it was all more straightforward without that guard, nobody had told him about any guard. Perhaps Toribio's memory failed him in this detail, and that was why he was so insistent.

'And who was it that acted as watchman in Hemingway's last years?'

Toribio opened his eyelids a bit further, trying to get his visitor into focus. He seemed to be making a supreme effort.

'You a bloody cop, or what?'

'No, no, I'm not a cop. I'm a writer.'

'Damn it all, you seem like a bloody cop then. And I like cops as much as a kick in the ass. I can't stand them.'

'Neither can I,' concurred Conde, without having to make much of an effort and without straying too far from the truth.

'Just as well . . . Look, I was locked up for three days because of a cop who caught me in an illegal cockfight. The bastard . . . As if there weren't still some big noises involved in cockfighting. Let's see, what was it you were asking me?'

'About the watchman. Who was it in the last few years?'

'Well, in the end, right at the end, when they

went off and Papa killed himself, it was someone called Iznaga, a huge black man, who was Raúl's cousin. But before that it had been Calixto, who used to do any job around the Finca, until one day he left . . .'

'People used to stay at the Finca for a long time, didn't they?'

'Of course they were going to stay – Papa paid well, really well. Nobody wanted to leave there. One day we worked it out and he alone used to support about thirty people . . .'

'And why did Calixto leave?'

'I don't know why. I do know how. One evening he and Papa were talking for hours up on the top floor of the tower. As if they didn't want anyone to hear them. And afterwards Calixto left. He even moved from San Francisco. Something pretty major must have happened between the two of them, because they had known each other for years, since before Calixto killed a guy and was sent to prison.'

Conde felt a buzz that he hadn't experienced since his days as a cop. Can it be true that you never stop being a cop, he asked himself, although he knew the answer: you never have the privilege of being an ex-anything, whether it's a cop, a sonofabitch, a queer or a murderer.

'What's the story behind that dead man, Toribio?'

The old man slowly swallowed as he rubbed his hands together.

'I really don't know, because Calixto was quite mysterious and he had some temper . . . What we did know was that he'd had a row in a bar and he killed a guy. He was put away for about fifteen years, and Papa gave him a job when he got out because he knew him from before.'

'And what became of Calixto?'

'I didn't see him again. Perhaps Ruperto did. Ruperto was the skipper of Papa's boat, and he used to get around Havana more. I think he once mentioned Calixto to me, but I can't remember.'

'Ruperto's still alive, isn't he?'

'Yes, he's something like fifteen years younger than me . . . But Calixto was older. So he . . .'

Toribio paused and Conde waited for a few

moments. Talking about so many dead people couldn't be much fun for the old man. He looked at his eyes, lost in deep thought, and decided to attack.

'Toribio, up there in the Vigía, did you ever, by any chance, hear talk of an FBI agent?'

The old man blinked.

'A what?'

'Someone from the American police. The one that's called the FBI . . .'

'Ah, the FBI. Hell. I know . . . Well no, not that I can remember, no.'

'Where was the cockpit at the Finca?'

'Just below the house, between the driveway and the garages. Beneath a mango tree . . .'

'An old mango tree, with white mangos?'

'Yes, that's the one . . .'

'Near the fountain?'

'More or less.'

Conde contained his feeling of delight. Without knowing what he was firing at he had hit an unexpected bull's eye.

'And what about you Toribio, why did you call

Hemingway "Papa" if he was such a bastard?'

The old man smiled. He had dark gums, speckled with white.

'He was the strangest guy in the world. He used to piss in the garden; he farted wherever he was. At times he adopted this posture, as if he was thinking, and he used to pick out his snot with his fingers and roll it into little balls. He couldn't stand people calling him "Sir". He was a better payer than other rich Americans. And he insisted on being called "Papa" . . . he said he was everybody's father.'

'What favours did you owe Hemingway?'

'Favours? None at all: I worked well and he paid me well, end of story. He said he was the best writer in the world and he had to have the best trainer of fighting cocks. That's why he apologised to me after we had the row.'

'Amongst all of you, who was the man Hemingway trusted most?'

'Raúl, no question about that. If Papa asked him to wipe his ass for him, Raúl wiped it for him.'

'Did you enjoy life at the Finca?'

'After the row, yes. He knew I was a man and

respected me . . . Besides, you used to see things there that made life worth living.'

'What sort of things?'

'Lots . . . but the one I can't forget is the morning I saw that American actress friend of his, who often used to stay at the Finca . . .'

'Marlene Dietrich?'

'I'm not sure, a young American girl . . .'

'Ava Gardner?'

'Look, he used to call her "my daughter" and I called her "La Gallega", the Spanish Girl, because she was very white and she had black hair. And one day I saw her swimming naked in the pool. Both of them, stark naked. I was looking for dry grass for a nesting-box and I turned to stone. La Gallega stood right on the edge of the pool and started to take off all her clothes. Until she just had her knickers on. And then she began to speak to him; he was already in the water. What a pair of tits . . . And before diving in, she took off her knickers. That was quite some daughter Papa had.'

'Were the knickers black?'

'How did you know that?' the old man asked, almost angrily.

'It's because I'm a writer. We writers know a few things, don't we? Was she good-looking?'

'Good-looking? What the fuck does that mean? More than good-looking: she was an angel, I swear on the memory of my mother, who really *was* an angel. That skin – and may God forgive me, but my prick started to have a life of its own, seeing La Gallega like that, stark naked, with that very smooth skin and her two fine tits and her reddish pubic hair, shining there . . . It was all too much . . . Then, when they started to play around in the pool, I left. That's a different story.'

'Yes, a different story. What about his wife?'

'Miss Mary must have known about Papa's fooling around. On one occasion he installed a little Italian princess he was crazy about in the Finca. He gave up fishing, cockfighting, writing, everything. He used to spend each day following her around like a horny dog, and when he spoke to us he was always in a filthy mood . . . But Miss Mary remained silent. When all's said and done, she was living like a queen.'

Conde lit another cigarette and closed his eyes: he tried to imagine Ava Gardner's striptease and felt his legs going weak. That wonderful image would soon be nothing, with Hemingway dead, Ava dead, and Tuzao heading for death. But the black knickers, would they be immortal?

'I'm off now Toribio, but before I go tell me – Hemingway, the man who killed lions and whatever else was around, even cocks, did he have the balls to kill a man?'

The old man shifted about restlessly in his seat, blinked and again focused on Conde.

'Look, you may be a writer, but you're also a cop. Don't fuck around with me . . . but I'll still answer your question. No, I don't think so: his style consisted of a lot of shouting around, a lot of posing with animals and a lot of showing off so that people would think he was a real man.'

'And he really was a bastard?'

'He really was. A man who kills a fighting cock just for the fun of it must be a real bastard. There are no two ways about it.'

𑀆𑀬 𑀒𑀭

He slung the Thompson over his shoulder and, overcoming the stiffness in his joints, knelt down and picked it up. Although he already had an idea of what it was, he shone his torch on it. The shield, the row of numbers and the three letters shone on the silvered metal badge, attached to a piece of leather. Like an animal alerted by the smell of danger, he looked around him and remembered what Raúl had told him about Black Dog's nervous state. Had an FBI agent been there? How else could that badge have got there, so close to the house, so far from the entrance? Were those bastards stalking him? He knew that since the war in Spain and his submarine-hunting, the federal agents had had him on their list. He even knew that Edgar Hoover himself had tried to accuse him of being a Communist back in the days of the McCarthy witch-hunts, but somebody had stopped him, saying that it was better to exclude an American hero like him from a hunt for Communists. But that badge, on his own property, sounded a warning to him. Of what?

He looked up and saw the lights of Havana in the distance, stretching down to the dark stain of the ocean. It was an elusive and unfathomable city, determined to live with its back to the sea, and about which he only had scraps of information, perhaps the least authentic scraps. He knew something about its poverty and its luxury; a lot about its bars and its cockpits; quite a lot about its fishermen and its sea; just enough about its pain and vanity. And nothing else, despite the many years that he had spent living beside it. It always happened like that with him: he had never known how to value, and almost never how to return the affection of those who really loved him. It was an old and unfortunate shortcoming, but it wasn't posturing or self-conscious, in fact he attributed it to the unsociable attitudes of his parents, those strange old people, with their lives wrapped up beneath a hypocritical puritanism, whom he could never love and who had ruined for ever his capacity to feel love in a simple, natural way.

Black Dog barked and broke his train of thought. He was barking in the dip in the slope that ran from the edge of the swimming-pool, almost at the outer edge of the Finca, and he was barking with an unusual insistence. The other two dogs, at the front gate, joined in the concert. Scanning the boundary of the property, Hemingway put the badge away in his shorts pocket and took hold of the machine gun. 'Come and look for your badge, you bastard, I'm going to take care of you,' he muttered, as he went down the slope and whistled to the animal. The barking stopped and Black Dog reappeared, wagging his tail, though growling.

'What's up, old thing, did you see him?' he asked him, as he noticed the grass trampled down on both sides of the fence. 'I know you're a ferocious watchdog . . . but I don't think that there's anyone here any more. The faggot got away. Let's go and see Calixto.'

He went back to the swimming-pool and took the short-cut between the casuarina trees that led to the main drive of the Vigía, avoiding the long detour that cars had to make. He felt comfortable under those proud and noble trees. They were like faithful friends: they had met in 1941, when he and Martha came to the Finca for the first time and he decided to buy it, already convinced that Havana was a good place for writing and that the Finca, so far from and yet so close to the city, seemed not just good, but ideal. And it really had turned out that way. That's why the fate of those trees had caused him so much concern when he landed in Normandy in 1944, as a devastating cyclone was crossing Havana. When he got back the following year and found that almost all his silent comrades were still standing, he could breathe easy; because that place, so good for writing, could also be a good place for dying, when the time came. But without its trees, the Finca would be worthless.

Thinking about death again took his mind off his discovery. He had already had the rare experience of being dead in the eyes of the rest of the world, when his plane had crashed near Lake Victoria during his second African safari. Like the character in Molière, it had given him the chance to find out what many of his friends and acquaintances thought of him. It wasn't pleasant to read the obituaries published in several newspapers and to discover how many more people didn't like him than he could have foretold. But he assumed that such harsh reactions were an inevitable consequence of his relationship with the world and a reflection of an old human habit: not to forgive other people's success. Anyway, that false death brought him a feeling of freedom, though from that moment onwards, the way in which he was to die became an obsession, particularly as the time to die young and heroically had now passed, and his abused body was beginning to deteriorate. From then on he had difficulty in passing water, problems with his sight and even worse ones with his hearing. And he would forget things that he used to know well. And he suffered badly from high blood pressure. And he had to restrict his intake of food and alcohol. And his old throat infection pursued him more ferociously . . . In the final analysis, death would relieve him of restriction and pain; he was only worried that it might also force him to interrupt certain areas of his work that he still wanted to complete. That's why, before it arrived, he had to see another bullfight in order to finish the rewriting of *Death in the Afternoon*, and he wanted to revise *Islands in the Stream* one more time, and finish that wretched *Garden of Eden*, so stalled and rambling. He also planned to sail once more between the coves of the north Cuban coast, to go up as far as Bimini, go back to Key West, surrounded by crooks and countless demijohns of rum and whisky. He also liked to toy with the idea that he could still make another safari to Africa, and even with the possibility of spending another autumn in Paris. Too many plans, quite possibly. What's more, he had to decide, before death arrived, whether or not he should cremate *A Moveable Feast*. It was a beautiful, sincere book but it said things that were too close to the truth, which would certainly be remembered in the future. A tiresome instinct had made him keep the manuscript, while awaiting some inspiration that would make its fate clear to him: either publish it or consign it to the fire.

Kitty Cannell, a friend of Hadley, his first wife, had shouted right in his face once: it disgusted her the way he turned against people who helped him, repaying them with ill-feeling, selfishness, malice and cruelty. Kitty must have been right. There was no reason for him to attack Gertrude Stein in order to evoke Paris and the years of hunger and work and happiness, even if the butch, deceitful old woman deserved it. And much less still poor Scott Fitzgerald, even if he couldn't bear that vulnerability of his, his inability to live and act like a man, always worried by that harpy Zelda's evil rumours about the size of his dick. And he no longer had any idea why he had attacked old Dorothy Parker, the forgotten Louis Bloomfield and that fool Ford Maddox Ford. Nevertheless, he had kept quiet about how his friendship with Sherwood Anderson ended, after the latter had given him letters, references and addresses that had opened the doors of precisely that post-war Paris which he needed to get to know. Writing that poor parody of his old master, just to get out of his contract with Anderson's publishers, had been an unworthy act, though his new publisher had paid him well for it. His subsequent decision that *The Torrents of Spring* would never be published again came too late to close the wound he had opened in the back of a man who had behaved so kindly and selflessly towards him.

Ten years before, when he had rejected the nomination as a Member of the American Academy of Arts and Letters, his reputation had grown. There was talk of his usual rebelliousness, his perpetual iconoclasm, his natural style of living and writing, far from academies and literary circles, between a Finca in Havana and a war in Europe. Things like this saved him from the McCarthyist fire into which the FBI and its larger-than-life boss, the abominable Hoover, wanted to cast him. What nobody imagined was that his refusal of the nomination was actually due to his inability to mix with other writers; to tolerate the presence of men like Faulkner and Dos Passos next to him. The conceited patriarch from the South had attacked him mercilessly in a vulnerable spot, since he had accused him of being a coward: Faulkner elegantly and disdainfully considered him the least failed of modern American writers, though the reason that he was the least failed was his greater artistic cowardice. He, who had freed the American language from all its euphemistic rhetoric and had dared to talk of 'balls' when the exact word needed was 'balls'. And what about the cowardice of Dos Passos, why hadn't he mentioned that? Fleeing from the Republican ranks in Spain when the cause needed him most had been the most cowardly of his acts in the proving ground of war. The whole business of putting the life of one person above the interests of a whole people was crazy, as was Dos Passos' statement that the death of the translator Robles was the work of Stalin. It's true that, in the name of a revolution of which he had taken charge, Stalin ended up agreeing terms with the Nazis, invading Finland and part of Poland, killing generals and writers, sending everyone who didn't submit to his plans to Siberia, and keeping the gold from the Spanish treasury and the money that many people – Hemingway himself included – had collected throughout the world for the Spanish Republic . . . but as for killing an insignificant translator like Robles? The feverish minds of writers such as Dos Passos disgusted him, and that was why Hemingway had preferred the company of simpler and truer men

– fishermen, hunters, bullfighters, fighters – with whom you could talk about bravery and courage. Besides, something inside him prevented him from being sincerely reconciled with those who had once been his friends: however much he tried, neither his mind nor his heart would allow it, and that inability to be reconciled felt like a punishment for his arrogance and the *machista* fundamentalism that governed so much of his life.

Anyway, he didn't want either writers or politicians in his company. And that's why he refused, increasingly, to talk about literature. If somebody asked him about his work, he'd just say, 'Work's going well' or perhaps 'I wrote four hundred words today.' It was meaningless to say anything else, since he knew that the further you go when you're writing, the lonelier you get. And in the end you learn that you must defend that solitude: talking about literature is a waste of time, and if you're alone it's much better, because that's how you should work, and because the time left for working gets less and less, and if you waste it you feel that you've committed a sin for which there is no forgiveness.

That's why he'd refused to travel to Stockholm to attend such a dull and worn-out ceremony as receiving the Nobel Prize. It was a pity that the prize could be awarded without being asked for, and that rejecting it could be considered an exaggerated gesture of bad taste: but that was what he wanted to do, since apart from the $36,000 which was so welcome, it didn't mean very much to him to have an award that people like Sinclair Lewis and Faulkner already had, and if he had turned it down his rebel's halo would have touched the stars. The only satisfaction of winning the prize was to count off on his fingers those authors who had not received it: Wolfe, Dos Passos, Caldwell, poor Scott, the bisexual Carson McCullers, prepared to display her sexual orientation beneath a baseball cap. And, of course, there was also the pleasure of being vindicated as a writer. But between that and buying a dress suit and travelling halfway around the world just to deliver a speech there was a chasm over which he just couldn't jump. He cited ill health due to his plane crashes in Africa, and when he received the cheque and the gold medal, he paid off debts, sent some money to Ezra Pound, who had just come out of mental hospital, and handed the medal itself to a Cuban journalist so that he could place it in the Chapel of Miracles of the Virgin of Charity of Cobre. It was a pretty gesture which gained excellent press coverage, and improved his standing with the Cubans, who are so romantic and sentimental, and also with the next life, all in one go.

'It was a good shot, wasn't it, Black Dog?'

The dog wagged his tail, but didn't look at him. Black Dog took his role as an effective guard-dog very seriously. Now, his attention was caught by an owl, which from the top of a royal palm tree sent out its hooting into the night. For the Cubans it was a bird of ill omen; he was sorry it was too dark for shooting – a burst from his Thompson would dismiss all the auguries possible in one go, especially the bad ones, perhaps even an FBI intruder. What could those bastards be snooping around for?

At the end of the short-cut through the trees the music could already be heard. Calixto was keeping himself company with a radio and the other two dogs on his night-watch duty. He couldn't understand that capacity of Cubans to spend hours on end listening to music, in particular those tearful *boleros* and Mexican *rancheras* that Calixto liked so much. In fact there were lots of things that he didn't understand about the Cubans.

आ ८

He saw her when she was already on the edge of the swimming-pool. She was wearing a fresh, flowery bath-robe and her hair was loose, falling around her shoulders. He thought her hair seemed lighter than he remembered and he once more enjoyed the perfect beauty of her face. She said something that he couldn't hear or didn't understand, perhaps on account of the noise that his own arms were making in the water. He moved them so as not to sink, and they felt heavy and almost not part of him. Then she took off her bathrobe. She wasn't wearing a swimsuit underneath, just a bra and a pair of knickers, black ones, made of revealing lace. The cups of the bra were provocative and he could see, through the lace, the pink aureole of her nipples. The erection he experienced was immediate, unexpected: it no longer happened to him in that sudden, vertical way, but he still enjoyed the feeling of swelling power. She looked at him and moved her lips, but he still couldn't hear her. His arms no longer had any weight and all that mattered to him was to watch her and enjoy the swelling of his penis, pointing at its target like a swordfish full of evil intent; he was naked, in the water. She stretched her hands round to her back and, with admirable female skill, unhooked the straps of her bra and revealed her breasts: they were round and full, crowned with dark pink nipples. His penis, overjoyed, warned him insistently of the speed with which things were happening. Although he tried, he couldn't call her: something prevented him from doing so. He did manage, however, to divert his eyes from her breasts to notice how, through the fine black fabric of her knickers, a deeper darkness could be glimpsed. Her hands were already at her hips, her fingers beginning to pull down the fine material, her pubic hair appearing, very black and shining, like the crest of a whirlwind that had its birth in her navel and exploded between her legs, and he couldn't see any more. Despite his efforts to contain himself he felt the warm semen gushing from him, aware of its oddly sweet smell.

'Oh, fuck,' he finally said, as an unexpected fit of conscience warned him that all his efforts to contain himself would be futile, and he allowed the remainder of his incontinence to burst out splendidly. Eventually he opened his eyes and looked at the ceiling: the image of Ava Gardner's nakedness lingered on his mind's eye at the instant she had revealed the advance guard of her Mount of Venus. Lazily he moved his hand down to feel the results of that journey to heaven. His fingers found his member, still hardened, covered with the lava of his eruption, and to fulfil the desire for physical satisfaction that held him in its grip he went to work with his hand, covered with the nectar of life, on the taut skin of his penis, which curved upwards like a grateful mongrel, and emitted a few more discharges into the air.

'Oh, fuck,' he repeated. Conde smiled, relaxed. His dream had been as satisfactory and lifelike as a fully consummated act of love and he had no regrets about it, except its brevity. He would have liked to prolong it for a couple of minutes more and know what it was like to screw Ava Gardner as she stood on the edge of the swimming-pool, and hear her whisper in his ear: 'Go on, Papa, go on', his hands gripping her buttocks and one of his fingers, the boldest and most daring one, making its way in through the back door of that enchanted castle.

The dream had caught him unawares after he had showered. Wanting to get to the bottom of the mystery, he had postponed his umpteenth reading of *A Catcher in the Rye*, Salinger's insubstantial, inexhaustible novel which, for several years now, had gripped his imagination, and decided instead to go through an old biography of Hemingway that he had picked up in the course of his business comings and goings. With the book under his arm, he opened all the windows, switched the fan on and stretched out naked on the bed. When he felt the rub of the sheet against his buttocks, the memory of Tamara, absent now for too long, gripped him and turned his scrotum into a swollen fruit: caught between the growing desire to make love with her and the fear that he never would again, fear had won out. And what if Tamara didn't come back? The mere thought of losing the one woman he didn't want to lose made him feel ill. He had already suffered too many losses to have to brace himself now for this one. 'Don't play such a dirty trick on me, Tamara,' he said aloud and opened the book. He wanted to relive the author's final years, delve into his fears and obsessions, find out what had caused him to place the barrel of his hunting shotgun into his mouth and pull the trigger. But he had hardly read fifteen pages when he'd been assailed by a malevolent drowsiness and was overcome by sleep, as if his forced abstinence and his obsession with a pair of black knickers belonging to Ava Gardner (which he hadn't even seen), had compelled him to sleep in order to give him an unexpected reward.

He was in such a mess that he had to go back

to the shower. The cold water purged him of filth and the residue of desire, and cleared his head so that he could clearly see the significance behind what he had read before falling asleep: it was his delusion that he was being pursued that had devastated Hemingway's intelligence in the final years of his life, and had perhaps been the main reason for his suicide. Two years prior to killing himself Hemingway had begun to sense that he was being determinedly followed and kept under surveillance, although he attributed this to the fact that he was suspected of tax dodging. Manolo felt this was a weak argument; he had a theory that there was something else, something being kept secret. His suspicion was reinforced by the mention of fifteen pages of FBI reports on Hemingway being censored 'on grounds of national security'. Records of Hemingway's activities had been kept ever since the days of the Spanish Civil War, and particularly since his adventures hunting German submarines during the 'Crook Factory' intelligence operation – more or less a bunch of drunken undesirables sailing on free fuel in a period of rationing. What must the

FBI and Hemingway have known about each other? What could that information have been that was so dramatic, capable of forcing one party to keep something secret in perpetuity and the other to feel himself under siege and pursuit? Could it be possible that the whole story revolved around that lost corpse and the FBI badge buried with it? Conde felt more and more that that badge with its three letters was an accusing finger in search of a suspect to point at. But his mind could not fully assimilate the idea that if Hemingway had ever actually killed a man, it should be a member of the FBI and in the sanctuary of his own private property.

Conde went to the kitchen in his underpants, prepared some coffee, lit a cigarette and looked at the cover of the biography, in which a Hemingway who was still solid and sure of himself looked out at him from a window of the Finca Vigía. 'Did you kill him or didn't you?' Conde asked. Whatever part the writer had played in the murder, that event seemed to have been the beginning of a terrible dénouement. Feeling himself hounded by the FBI and convinced that poverty and even cancer were lying in wait for him, the hard man finally weakened, and like any poor guy assailed by psychosis and depression he ended up in a clinic where, to make him forget his supposed delusions and rampant obsessions (for God's sake, Conde trembled, what on earth is a writer without his obsessions?) they administered a series of fifteen electroshocks capable of frying any brain; they filled him up to the neck with tranquillisers and antidepressants; they forced him to follow an inhuman diet, and they initiated his definitive and brutal collapse. It wasn't strange that a man who was always so proud of the injuries he had acquired in war and adventure should conceal his name on checking into the Mayo Clinic for the first time. There wasn't a touch of heroism in that hospital stay, just the proof of a devastating process that was demolishing even the last vestige of that man's fortune: his intelligence.

The feeling of impotence and helplessness that the old writer must have experienced moved Conde in an alarming way. And he thought, there's no satisfaction in this. It was like fighting for the crown against a punchbag: that lifeless bag could resist some blows, perhaps several, but it was unable to respond to such an aggressive attack. In this case, at least, he preferred the big, dirty American, foulmouthed and drunken, arrogant and bullying, who while he invented epic stories about himself, wrote stories about losers and earned thousands of dollars with them – enough to have a yacht, the Finca in Havana, hunting trips in Africa and holidays in Paris and Venice. He wanted to square up to the thundering god, and not to the enfeebled, forgetful old man who was denied everything that he had once been in life and everything he had most loved, even alcohol and literature. And you don't mess with that, concluded Conde, who, because of his own weaknesses and beliefs, couldn't help feeling solidarity with writers, crazy people and drunkards.

The worst thing was that Hemingway had devoted what was left of his tortured and terminal lucidity to blaming himself for his failures and limitations. In the final conversations he had had when still of sound mind, there were signs of a growing sadness for having failed in the construction of his own myth, culminating in the point at which he asked his publishers to remove all reference to his heroic or adventurous deeds from the covers of his books. His sexual inadequacy in his final years had also tortured him, especially when he'd discovered that when caught between Adriana Ivancich and his frustration he had to opt for the latter, and that it was preferable to watch the red-haired, provocatively youthful, Valerie Danby-Smith walk past him, without pouncing . . . But what was more, he'd been haunted by a feeling of guilt at having preferred life to literature, adventure to creative engagement. This meant he had betrayed his own ideal of total dedication to his art. In the world he was celebrated and regarded as a permanent exhibit of muscles and scars, capable of posing among models from *Vogue* and advertising a brand of gin, of turning his house into a macho tourist stop for marines on their way through Havana, rather than how he truly felt, as a man living in the shadow of a futile reputation more suitable for an action hero on perpetual safari than a man dedicated to the battle with words, a resilient enemy that was immune to bullets. And now the champion lacked the courage to stand up to life in the world he had created: in short, he himself was a loser. Then he'd begun to talk about suicide – he of all people, who had stigmatised the memory of his father when he had opted for death at his own hands. The palate: the palate is the weakest point in the head. A shot in the palate can't fail, and with his Mannlicher Schoenauer 256 in his mouth he'd begun to rehearse his own end, to get publicity for it before it even happened.

In his years as a policeman Conde had liked to get involved in cases like this one, in which he immersed himself to the point of losing breath and almost consciousness; in which he enveloped himself to the extent that they became his own skin. After all, he had been a good cop at one time, despite his dislike of firearms, violence, repression and the legal authority granted to crush and manipulate others through fear and all the macabre mechanisms of the apparatus of power. But now, he was clear about this, he was a goddamn private detective in a country with neither detectives nor private people; he felt like a bad metaphor for a strange reality. He was, he had to admit, just one more poor guy living out his little life, in a city full of ordinary guys and dull existences, without any poetic ingredient and increasingly deprived of dreams. That's why the ever-present possibility of never reaching the truth about the murder didn't even bother him: at this stage it already seemed impossible to know if Hemingway was or wasn't the killer, and in some far recess of his mind Conde was already certain that the only reason he needed to know was in order to satisfy his nagging sense of justice. In this story everything had come too late, and the most crucial thing was that the last person to arrive had been him, Mario Conde.

The dog's insistent barking roused him from the depths of his musings. He did up his trousers while shouting 'I'm coming, old man', and he finally opened the door onto the porch.

'Good evening. It's been a long time . . .'

His dog stood up on its hind legs and rested its front paws on Conde's thighs, still barking, demanding something more than reproach. Its hair, originally white and straight, looked like brown molasses, and Conde felt its stodgy consistency as he stroked the animal's head and ears.

'For God's sake, Garbage, you're a fucking mess. You know, some love affairs can be fatal.' The dog, grateful for the attention, licked his master's hand thoroughly. This was an old habit Conde had allowed ever since that hurricane-filled evening when he and Garbage had first met in the street. It was love at first sight, and he decided to take him home. In the same way they had agreed, by a happy mutual accord, from that day onwards Conde would play the part of master: he would feed Garbage whenever it was possible and he would wash him when it was unavoidable, while, for his part, the dog brought affection and gratitude to the relationship, but not the freedom inherited through his genes as a street mongrel.

'You're a good dog. A bit shameless, you don't give a damn, you wander off whenever you feel like it, but your heart's in the right place . . . Come on, let's see what I've got for you.'

In the fridge he found a bit of rice, the remains

of a chickpea stew and a few chunks of mackerel left in a tin. Conde tipped it all into the dog's bowl, mixed it up and took it out onto the porch, once again urged on by the animal's barking.

'For Christ's sake, old man, hold on a bit. There you go, hope you enjoy it.'

With satisfaction, Conde watched the dog eating, right down to the very last grain of rice. Then, with less urgency, Garbage drank some water and, all in the same movement, dropped onto one side and fell asleep.

'What a wanderer . . . See you tomorrow,' said the man and closed the door. Dressed and scented as if he were in search of a girlfriend, Conde went out into the fumes of the street. He was heading towards his friend Skinny Carlos's house, because he needed to communicate his interrupted dreams and his musings, to say nothing of filling his belly, and he knew no better listener in the world than Skinny, nor any better gastronomic magic than that of Josefina.

Despite the heat, he found the streets teeming with people. They all seemed trapped by an anxiety that could only be relieved through shouting, violent gestures and resentful glances. Life goaded them on and flung them into an everyday war that took place in the open air and on all fronts. While some sold anything you could imagine, others bought, or dreamed of buying. While some expended their last drop of sweat pedalling a bicycle, others smiled coolly from behind their chilled cans of beer, on sale only for dollars. While some came out of the local church, others crept from an illegal gambling dive . . . Two young girls in skimpy black dresses were hitching a lift to the city, ready for the physical demands of their night work, also paid for in dollars. A destitute one-legged man was begging from passers-by. Two boys were taking a fighting dog for a walk, dreaming of the money they would earn thanks to the animal's teeth. A black man, well-built and loaded down with gold chains and crucifixes and medals of the Virgin tangled in harmony with primitive *santería* necklaces, was kicking the punctured tyre of a beaten-up 1954 Oldsmobile while pouring out obscenities . . . In the midst of this maelstrom

Conde tried in vain to find where he belonged. For the first time in his more than forty years of life the streets of this district felt unfamiliar to him; offensive, hostile. The devastating reality that he saw before him had been slumbering for some years, or simmering in the darkness; now it was about to erupt, and the clouds of smoke it was giving off were warning signs. It wasn't essential to be a cop, a private detective or even a writer to realise that it would make no difference to anyone in those streets if Hemingway had or hadn't killed a guy who was hell-bent on fucking up his life. Life – and death – was heading in a different direction, far removed from literature and the unreal peace of Finca Vigía.

Black Dog and the other two dogs moved about nervously, sniffing around the boundaries of the Finca.

'Something's the matter with these dogs,' he said.

'They're restless,' agreed Calixto. They had sat down on a fallen tree trunk beside the path that led to the house. From there, through the wooden gates, they could see the road that went to the town, with its houses of rotten wood and their tile roofs blackened by years of sun and rain. At the end, beyond Victor's bodega, the swift movement of cars moving along the Carretera General could be heard. Calixto had turned off the radio when he heard his boss nearby. He knew how much he hated his taste in music.

'Have you seen anything strange?'

'No, nothing. Just now I had a look out back . . . And what about you Ernesto, did you see anything?'

'No, but I found this next to the swimming-pool,' and he took the FBI badge out of his pocket.

'What's that?'

'It belongs to the American police. I don't know how the hell it got here.'

Calixto shifted uncomfortably.

'The American police?'

'You haven't done anything, have you, Calixto?'

'No, of course not. Since I came out I've been happier than a baby at the breast. Even more so now that things are so tough here. No.'

'Well then, how did this bloody thing find its way to the swimming pool?'

'I've been here since ten past nine, and I haven't seen anything.'

'I think they've got me under surveillance. They must do.'

'Why did you bring out that lump of metal?' Calixto pointed to the Thompson, which Hemingway was holding against his legs, the butt resting on the ground.

'I don't know why I brought it out. I was going to put it away in the tower . . .'

'It must just be a spot of bother with the revolutionaries. Nobody's got you under surveillance, Ernesto. Why would they want to?'

'Don't forget that they've already searched the house once.'

'But that was the police here, because of the

firearms. These ones are different.' He pointed to the badge. 'What can they be after?'

'I've no idea,' he admitted.

More and more there were things that he didn't understand or found that he had never understood. He also noted with a certain frequency how he was forgetting things. Ferrer Machuca, his doctor, had prescribed him vitamins, advised him to give up alcohol and confessed to him smilingly:

'At times I have the same problem. I forget the slightest thing . . . It's because we're getting old and life's too hectic for us.'

'But there are things I don't forget,' he said.

Calixto looked at him and smiled: he knew his boss's way of saying things out of the blue.

'What things?'

'Things.'

He couldn't forget his first visit to the Floridita with his friend Joe Russell. They were returning from a disastrous fishing expedition and just wanted to drown themselves in alcohol, and Joe took him to the Floridita, where they met Calixto, whom he already knew because of his frequent trips to Key West. He was always grateful to Joe for that visit, because he had fallen in love with the bar at first sight: he at once preferred it to the other bars in Havana. In those days the Floridita was an establishment that was open to the street, with large fans in the ceiling and a beautiful dark wooden bar to lean on, where you drank good rum at reasonable prices, and where you ate delicious prawns, fresh and tasting of the sea. What's more, you could find out everything that was happening in the city: the whores and journalists who comprised its usual clientèle took it upon themselves to bring the other customers up to date. Listening to stories about local politics, smuggled alcohol and people, about the gangs that operated in the city, the idea for *To Have and Have Not* was born. It was there, too, that he heard a couple of years later that Calixto was in prison for having killed a man, and he was sorry about this, since the alcohol smuggler had always seemed like a good guy to him, someone who could tell wonderful stories. Then, when he moved to Havana once and for all, he became a regular at the Floridita, along with his friends the whores and his journalist colleagues, and in honour of all the drinks downed there by him there was now a shiny metal plaque commemorating his faithfulness to the bar and his status as a Nobel Prize winner. As a gesture of gratitude to that place where they made the best daiquiri in Cuba, where a man could drink for hours without being bothered and where you could chat free from the aggression of the music without which Cubans seemed unable to live, he had chosen the Floridita as the setting for a large section of *Islands in the Stream*, a painfully autobiographical novel which he had put away in a drawer when he completed the last page.

Finding a place like that had been a bit of luck, since it had saved him the necessity of looking for other places where he could find out what he wanted to know about Havana. There, and in Cojímar and in San Francisco de Paula, he learned everything he needed to know about a city: how they ate, how they drank, how the people loved, how they fished and how they struggled with everyday poverty. He wasn't interested in anything else, since he was sure that it was all the same in Paris, New York or Havana.

To start with, the social life of Havana seemed empty and pretentious to him, and from the outset he refused to participate in it: he didn't accept invitations nor did he allow the local celebrities into the Finca. What's more, he scarcely visited the homes of his countless Cuban friends and kept himself apart from all the local problems that didn't affect him directly. The few exceptions that he had permitted he handled on his own terms, like the event organised by some rich Cuban brewers which he'd only agreed to attend if he could bring with him all his fishermen friends from Cojímar, who that night ate and drank thanks to Papa's fame.

He hadn't mixed with the island's writers and artists either, firstly because he didn't want to have any more writer friends, and secondly because most of the Cuban writers, with a couple of exceptions, didn't interest him either as people or creators. His universe of literary and cultural preferences was already established, and the little world of local scribblers could become a nightmare if he gave them a chance to become close to him. Too many full-time drunks, too many Frenchified dilettantes, too many eccentrics with pretensions of being island visionaries were swarming over the tropical Parnassus in which, as in all such places, there were more enemies than friends, more detractors than admirers, more envious people than sympathisers, more people who said they were writers than people capable of writing, more opportunists, creeps, bloodsuckers and sons of whores, than people devoted honestly and simply to exerting themselves for literature. Just like in New York and Paris. He knew some Cuban writers through their works and some lectures he had attended, particularly that crazy Serpa and the unbearable Novas Calvo, but he knew that he was capable of extracting from Cuba the literary material with which he wished to work without the need to share ideas and readings with his fellow writers. On top of that, he knew only too well how many of them criticised him for his distant, status-conscious attitude. Some of them did it out of envy, others out of malice, and some because he had been rude to them. But he maintained that not mixing with them had been one of his life-saving flashes of inspiration. After all, you could live in Cuba without having read its writers. You could even manage to become the President of the Republic.

'What do you think of me, Calixto?'

The man looked at him for an instant.

'I don't understand you, Ernesto.'

'Am I an arrogant American?'

'Who ever said such a dreadful thing?'

He was indignant that they should have accused him of living in Cuba because it was cheaper and because he was like all Americans, superficial and arrogant, going around the world buying with their dollars whatever was for sale. But the latest accounts drawn up by Miss Mary showed how he had spent almost a million dollars on the island over about twenty years, and he knew that a major part of that money had gone in paying the thirty-two Cubans who depended upon him for their livelihood. On more than one occasion, in order to rile the backbiters, he had stated to the press that he felt like a Cuban; that in fact he was just another

Cuban, a mongrel Cuban, he said, as mongrel as Black Dog and his other dogs; and he took this strategy still further when he decided to hand over his Nobel Prize medal to the Virgin of Charity of Cobre. She was the patroness of Cuba and of the fishermen of Cojímar, and there was nobody better to look after a medal which owed so much to some simple men who nonethless had given him the story of a fisherman who spent eighty-four days struggling in the Gulf Stream without capturing a fish, because he was completely out of luck.

Although he would really have preferred to live in Spain, nearer the wine, the bulls and the streams teeming with trout, the dreadful outcome of the Civil War had cast him up on this island. If he was certain of one thing, it was that he didn't want to live either under a Fascist dictatorship or in his own country. Cuba represented a satisfactory alternative and he was grateful for having been able to write several of his books there, and that it had provided him with several stories and characters. But that was all: the rest of it was a convention, a transaction, and it annoyed him now, though only now, that under the euphoric effects of alcohol he had ever pretended that he felt Cuban or even was Cuban.

'You know what I'm most sorry about?'

'What?'

'Having spent so long in Cuba and never having fallen in love with a Cuban woman.'

'You have no idea what you've missed out on,' said Calixto with conviction, and smiled, 'or what you've spared yourself.'

'Do you like being Cuban, Calixto?'

'I don't understand what the hell you're saying today, Ernesto.'

'Don't listen to me. This business has got me worried,' and he held up the FBI badge again. He still had it in his hand.

'You mustn't worry about it. I'm here. Raúl told me that he would have a look around later on . . .'

'Yes, you and Raúl are here. But tell me something: is it easy or difficult to kill a man?'

Calixto became nervous. He preferred not to talk about some things from the past.

'It was easy for me, too easy. We had put away

a lot of booze, the guy went too far, he drew his knife and I shot him. Just like that.'

'Other people say it's difficult.'

'What do you think? What was it like when you killed people?'

'Who said I killed anyone?'

'I don't know, people, you yourself . . . As you've been in so many wars. People kill each other in wars.'

'That's true,' and he stroked his Thompson, 'but I didn't. I've done a lot of killing, too much I think, but I've never killed a man. Although I think I'm capable of it . . . But then, if someone messes with you, you'd be capable of . . .'

'Don't talk to me about that, Ernesto.'

'Why not?'

'Because you don't deserve to be messed with by anyone . . . And because you're my friend and I'm going to protect you, aren't I? But it can't be much fun to die in prison.'

'No, it can't be much fun. Forget everything we've said.'

'When I left prison, I promised myself two

things: that I wouldn't have a drop to drink again and that I wouldn't set foot in a prison cell again.'

'You really haven't had a drop to drink again?'

'Not a drop.'

'But it was better before. When you drank rum you used to tell wonderful stories.'

'You're the teller of stories here, not me.'

He looked at Calixto and was amazed all over again by the complete darkness of his hair.

'But that's my problem: I need to tell stories, but I can't manage it any more. I always had a bag full of good stories and now I walk around with an empty bag. I rewrite old things because I can't think of anything new. I'm washed up, horribly washed up. I thought that old age was completely different. Do you feel old?'

'At times, yes, very old,' confessed Calixto. 'But what I do then is I start to listen to Mexican music, and I remember that I always thought that when I was old I would go back to Veracruz and live there. That helps me.'

'Why Veracruz?'

'It was the first place I visited outside Cuba.

I used to listen to Mexican music there. Over there Mexicans listen to Cuban music, women are beautiful and the food's good. But I know I'm not going to go back to Veracruz; I'll die here, as an old man, without ever having another drink.'

'You've never talked to me about Veracruz before.'

'We've never talked about old age before.'

'Yes, that's true,' he admitted. 'But there's still time to go back to Veracruz . . . Anyway, I'd better get off to bed now.'

'You sleeping well?'

'Bloody badly. But tomorrow I want to write. Although I can't think of anything, I must write. I'm off. Writing is my Veracruz.'

He smiled at Calixto and they shook hands. Then he used his machine gun to help him get to his feet. He stood up and looked towards the Finca. There was no breeze and the silence was dense.

'Let me have the gun, Ernesto.'

Calixto had also got to his feet, using a stick. Hemingway turned round.

'No,' he replied.

'What if the cops come around?'

'We'll talk to them. Nobody's going to go to prison, least of all you.'

'I'm going to search the Finca.'

'I don't think you need to. The person who left this has already gone.'

'Just in case,' insisted Calixto.

'Fine, Well, see you tomorrow. Come on, Black Dog.'

Slowly, with his old man's walk, he started to move up the short slope that led to the house. Black Dog went at his side, imitating his way of walking. Calixto watched him moving away and went back to the gate. He put the radio on, but no longer felt like enjoying *boleros* by Augustín Lara or *rancheras* by José Alfredo Jiménez. He switched it off and watched the calm night in the Finca.

'Yes, that was me, and of course I remember. That was the last time I saw Papa.'

The morning was still fresh, although there wasn't a hint of a breeze. A local boy had told him that Ruperto was to be found near the jetty in the river and, after asking a couple of fishermen, he found him beneath an almond tree, sitting on a stone, leaning back against the trunk with a huge unlit cigar in his mouth, gazing at the little wood that rose up on the opposite bank of the river. If he was fifteen years younger than Tuzao, he must be about ninety. However, he looked much younger, or at any rate less old. Conde corrected his initial opinion: a strong old man of eighty, wearing a straw hat, obviously expensive and hailing from some distant place.

After greeting him, Conde told him that he needed to speak to him.

'You want to interview me?' asked the old man, unenthusiastically, without removing the cigar from his mouth.

'No, just to chat for a while.'

'You sure about that?' His lack of enthusiasm was replaced by suspicion.

'I'm sure. Look, I'm unarmed . . . I want to know if something I think happened to me years ago could really have happened, or if it wasn't possible,' and he told him about his memory of the day on which he had seen Hemingway get off the *Pilar* in Cojímar cove and say goodbye to a man who must have been Ruperto himself.

'He turned up at my house at about midday, without warning, and as soon as I saw him I knew that something was wrong with him, but knowing him as I did, I didn't even ask. We just greeted each other and he said that I should get ready, we were going out to sea.'

'"Shall I bring lines and bait?" I asked him.

'"No, Rupert, we're going for a boat trip."

'He always used to call me Rupert and I called him Papa.'

The old man raised his arm and pointed.

'The *Pilar* was anchored out there.'

Conde followed the direction of his hand and saw the sea, the river and a few weather-beaten fishing boats.

'When did that happen, Ruperto?'

'On 24 July 1960. I remember that because the next day he got onto a plane and never came back.'

'Did he know he wasn't coming back?'

'I think he did. Because of what he said to me.

'"I'm washed up and I don't think there's anything they can do about it," he said. "And I'm frightened about what's going to happen."

'"What's the matter, Papa?"

'"The doctors don't want me to go, but I'm off to Spain. I've got to see some bullfights in order to finish my book. After that they're going to admit me to hospital. Then I don't know what's going to happen . . ."

'"But going into hospital doesn't mean the end."

' "That depends, Rupert. For me, I think it does."

'"Do you feel ill?"

'"Come off it, Rupert, are you blind? Can't you see I'm losing weight, that I've turned into an old man in just a couple of years?"

'"But we're both old men."

'"But I look the elder," and he smiled. But it was a sad smile.

'"You shouldn't pay too much attention to what doctors say. Ferrer is a Galician, and all Galicians are idiots. That's why they're almost all fishermen." We both laughed, and we meant it now. "And when you get better, will you come back?"

'"Yes, of course I will. But if I don't get better, I'm going to leave word that this boat is yours. Someone will give you the document of ownership. The only condition is that you don't sell it while you've still got a peso for food. If things get that bad, then sell it."

'"I don't want anything, Papa."

'"But I do. I don't want this boat sailed by anybody but you."

'"If that's the case I'll look after it."

'"Thanks, Ruperto."'

'Did he always talk to you about his affairs?' asked Conde.

'At times he did.'

'Did he ever tell you that he had problems with the FBI?'

'Not that I can remember, no. Well, yes . . .
He got angry with them when they put an end to
our search for German submarines in 1942. It was
an order that came from on high. But after that, no
he didn't.'

'And what else happened that day?'

'We sailed out to sea, cut the engines once we
were in the Gulf, where he liked fishing, and Papa
sat down in the stern and looked out to sea. That
was where he told me that he was washed up and
that he was frightened. I got a bit scared, because
Papa wasn't the kind of man to get frightened. He
really wasn't. After about an hour he asked to go
back to Cojímar and I realised that his eyes were
red. That's when I got really scared. I'd never
imagined that a man like him could cry.

'"Don't worry, I just got a bit emotional. I
was remembering what a good time we've had here,
fishing and drinking. Joe Russell introduced me to
this place thirty years ago."

'When we reached Cojímar you saw what
happened: we anchored, he got off, and we hugged
each other.'

'"Look after yourself, Ruperto."

'"Come back soon, Papa. That sea's full of fish . . ."'

'Were you surprised that he killed himself?' Conde asked, looking the old fisherman in the eye.

'No, not very. He was no longer himself, and I think that he didn't like the person he'd become.'

Conde smiled at Ruperto's conclusion. It seemed to him to be the most intelligent and likely one that he had heard or read concerning the writer's fate. And he understood that even as he was getting to know Hemingway and his troubles a bit better each day, the possible pathways to the truth remained blocked. Ruperto's gratitude to the man was insuperable, as was that of Tuzao, who skilfully concealed his love for his boss behind the statement that he was a real bastard: but a real bastard who had paid him well, who had taught him to read and who had left him a fortune in fighting cocks. Were these the favours which those two men owed him?

'Nice hat,' observed Conde.

'Miss Mary sent it to me with some Americans who came to interview me. It's a genuine panama hat, look.'

And he showed Conde the maker's label, hidden inside it.

'Someone told me you charged for interviews . . .'

'You know why? There are so many people coming to bother me that I have to.'

'It's a good way of earning a living. Better than fishing.'

'And easy: because I even tell them lies. Americans will swallow anything.'

'Would Hemingway?'

'No, Papa wouldn't. I couldn't tell him a lie.'

'Was he a good guy?'

'He was like God for me . . .'

'Tuzao says that he was a real bastard.'

'And did he tell you that he used to steal the best cockerel eggs from Papa and sell them to other fighting cock breeders? When Raúl found out about this and told Papa, they came to blows and Papa kicked him out of the Finca. Later on, Toribio swore to Papa that he wouldn't steal another egg from him, and he was forgiven.'

Conde smiled: he was among trained tigers. Each of them sorted out his own world in the best way he could and hid his mistakes. At least Toribio's had been found out. Or were there more?

'Raúl would do anything for Hemingway, wouldn't he?'

'Yes, anything.'

'I would like to have talked to Raúl . . . Did Hemingway kick any other employee out of the Finca?'

'Yes, there was a gardener who used to cut his trees down, and someone else . . . He couldn't bear his trees being pruned. But anyway, what are you trying to find out with all these questions?'

'Something that you're never going to tell me.'

'If you want me to say something bad about Papa, you're out of luck. Look, when I worked with him, I lived better than the other fishermen, and after he died, thanks to him, I still live well and even wear a panama hat. You know, the last thing I want to be is ungrateful.'

'Of course, I know. But there's going to be a real problem for Hemingway . . . A corpse has turned up at the Finca. The bones of a man who was killed forty years ago. He died of two gunshot wounds. And the police think that it was Hemingway who did it. To complicate matters further, an old FBI badge was found near the body. If they say Hemingway did it, he's going to be covered with shit. From head to toe.'

Ruperto remained silent. He seemed to be processing the alarming information provided by his strange visitor. His lack of obvious reaction warned Conde that he had sunk his spear into soft flesh.

'Who are you exactly? What is it you want?'

'As people put it so nicely, I'm a dick dressed in plain clothes. I was a cop before, although no less of a dick for that. And now I'm trying to be a writer, although I'm still the same dick and I earn my living by selling old books. Your Papa was very important for me, years ago, when I started writing. But then he lost his magic. I began to find out about the things he did to other people, I began to understand the character he was projecting, and I stopped liking him. But if I can prevent them pinning something on him that he didn't do, then I'll do it. It doesn't amuse me in the slightest that they should try to stitch up someone just for the sake of it, and I don't think that you would like that either. You're an intelligent man and you know the consequences that a dead body could bring.'

'Yes,' said Ruperto, and for the first time he took the cigar out of his mouth. He launched a sticky, brown blob of spittle that skidded over the dry earth.

'Who still survives out of the most trusted employees at the Finca?'

'As far as I know, just Toribio and me. Oh, and there's also the Galician, Ferrer, his doctor friend, but he lives in Spain now. He went back as soon as Franco died.'

'What about Calixto, the watchman?'

'He must be dead as well. He was older than me . . . but since he left the Finca I haven't heard any more about him.'

Conde lit a cigarette and looked out to sea.

Even beneath the almond tree he began to feel the heat of a day that was threatening to be hellish.

'Did Calixto leave or did Hemingway kick him out?'

'No, he left.'

'Why?'

'That's something I don't know.'

'But you do know Calixto's story, don't you?'

'What people used to say about him. That he had killed a man.'

'And Hemingway used to trust him?'

'I think so. They had been friends since before Calixto had had his problem.'

'And nobody knows where Calixto got to when he left the Finca? He must have been well paid there.'

'I once heard he had gone off to Mexico. He was very keen on everything Mexican.'

Conde assimilated that information carefully. If it were true it could be very significant.

'So far away? Would he be running away from something, by any chance?'

'I don't know that either . . .'

'But I bet you know when he went?'

Ruperto thought about this for a few moments. Just seeing him thinking about it Conde realised that the old man knew the date, but he was making other more complicated calculations, perhaps more dangerous ones. He eventually spoke.

'If my memory serves me right, it was at the beginning of October 1958. I know this because a few days later Papa went to the United States to join Miss Mary, who was already over there . . .'

'Remember anything else about that story?'

'Nothing else. What else am I going to remember?' he protested, and Conde felt that he was on the defensive.

'Ruperto,' said Conde, and stopped. He drew on his cigarette and considered his words carefully, 'Is there nothing else that you can tell me and that will help me to find out who the dead man at the Finca Vigía is and who killed him?'

The old man, once more with his cigar in his mouth, looked him in the eye.

'No.'

'A pity,' he said as he got to his feet and felt

how the rust of life was seizing up his knees. 'That's fine, don't tell me anything. But I know that you know something. This dick you see before you knows a thing or two . . . oh, and Ruperto, I love the hat.'

Conde knew the process: prejudices were like thorns in your hand and hunches struck you like a prickling feeling in the stomach, sharp and uncomfortable. But they both worked like seeds, and only if they fell on fertile ground could they grow and turn into painful certainties. And now Conde was certain that between the writer Ernest Hemingway and Hemingway's old acquaintance Calixto Montenegro, former alcohol smuggler, convicted murderer and employee at the Finca between 1946 and 1958, there existed some hidden link, different in some way from the relationship of grateful dependency which the writer had managed to forge with the rest of his workers. And while he made his way towards the centre of Cojímar, with the image of a glass of rum in his mind, the certainty grew, surprising him by the pain it caused. It was a hot, aggressive pain, and although he hadn't felt it for eight years, Conde was experiencing it now at full strength. At long last, as sharp and deep as a toreador's dagger, he felt one of the most delightful hunches he'd ever had, since it had a strictly literary origin.

After a double shot of rum and before catching a bus back to Havana, he achieved the miracle of finding a public telephone, in a little newspaper stall. More miraculous still, he reached the telephone exchange at the first attempt, and was put through to Inspector Palacios.

'What's up, Conde? I was on my way out.'

'Good job I caught you. I need you to make a call for me before you leave.'

'Get on with it, what's eating you?'

'I've really got a hunch now, Manolo.'

'Damn you,' responded Manolo, since he was only too well aware of the complexities of the case.

'It's a good one, one of the best I think . . . Look, phone the *Biblioteca Nacional* and tell them to give me all the books I ask for and to do it quickly. You know how long those bastards take over things and how cagey they are about certain books . . .'

'What are you looking for? If you don't mind letting me in on it . . .'

'A date. But I'll tell you all about it later on.'

'Well I've also got some things to tell you about. I'm off to a meeting now, but I'm going to be at Finca Vigía at about two o'clock. Shall we meet there?'

'Hey, I haven't got an outboard motor up my arse.'

'Look, just to show you how much I love you: at 1.30 you'll have a car with a driver waiting for you at the entrance to the library,' announced the Inspector. 'There have been developments, so we'll meet at the Finca. Hey, smartarse, don't go stealing any library books,' and with that he hung up.

At the height of summer, with the students on holiday, the *Biblioteca* breathed an atmosphere capable of calming Conde's anxieties. Moreover, submerging himself among books, ready to look for something that perhaps nobody else had ever sought in the works and life of Hemingway, gave him a pleasant sensation, unique to incurable bibliophiles. At moments like this Conde enjoyed the idea that books could talk and take on a life all their own. He knew that his love for these objects, to which he owed his living now and from which over the years he had derived a singular happiness, was one of the most important things in his life, a life in which there remained ever fewer important things. He began to count them: friendship, coffee, cigarettes, rum, making love from time to time – ay, Tamara, ay, Ava Gardner – and literature. And books, of course, he added at the end.

At the request counter he found that the order from on high to attend to all his requests as quickly as possible had brought results. Something, at least, seemed to be working on the island. To his surprise Conde discovered that although the library's catalogue held almost all Hemingway's narrative works and journalism, there was hardly anything about his life. Nevertheless, he filled in forms requesting all the literature on him published in English and Spanish and asked for it all to be brought to him at once. In any case his search had a specific target: the month of October 1958.

With three biographies and four critical

studies spread out in front of him, Conde lit a cigarette, breathed in until his lungs were filled with smoke, and plunged into his task like a diver. He began with the biographies, looking through their final chapters. One of them jumped from the Nobel Prize to the publication in *Life* of 'The Dangerous Summer' in 1960, without spending any time on what the writer did in Cuba in 1958. Another one, which had a lot of photos in it, only briefly mentioned his stay in Havana that year. However, Conde paused for a few minutes to look at the pictures, many of which were unknown to him. They showed the familiar figure far from the great settings of his life: old photos in which he appeared with his sisters or his mother, who'd insisted on dressing him as a girl; images of everyday life at the Finca Vigía, during some meals, meetings with his sons, gestures of affection towards Mary Welsh, the cats of the house and a dog called Black Dog, who looked at the camera with intelligent eyes; memorials of happy times with Hadley and Pauline, his first two wives and the mothers of his three children, and portraits of the old patriarch, bearded and grey-haired, apparently very tired, so similar to the dirty Santa Claus Conde had watched walk past him that day at the cove in Cojímar. Hemingway looked more human in those photographs, more of a real person than he'd ever seemed to him before. It was the third biography that really hit home: according to its author, at the beginning of October 1958 Hemingway had interrupted the writing of *The Garden of Eden*, the unsatisfactory old narrative started in the '40's which he was then redrafting as a novel, and on the 4th boarded a plane for the United States, to join his wife and complete the purchase of land in Ketchum, where he would build his last house. Bells were beginning to toll.

Two of the critical studies, published before 1986, when the definitive edition of *The Garden of Eden* came out, hardly mentioned the existence of that then-unknown work. The third one did speak of it, but just said that it had been started in Paris in 1946 and continued in Havana in 1958, when the writer had postponed his revision and enlargement of *Death in the Afternoon* pending a journey to Spain for the new bullfighting season. According to the author of the essay, those seem to have been difficult days for Hemingway, since his illnesses were beginning to besiege him and writing was becoming a difficult, almost agonising, exercise. But it was the final critical study that caused Conde to tremble: on going through the manuscripts taken from Cuba by Mary Hemingway, the author of this piece had discovered that the last page of that novel that the writer would leave unpublished at his death was dated Havana, 2 October 1958, with a now almost invisible marginal note in Hemingway's hand. The bells began to toll louder.

When Conde looked at his watch, he discovered that it was already five past two. He took the books to the counter at the double, thanked the librarian and ran towards the exit. A young man dressed in civilian clothes was cleaning the windscreen of a car that shone under the intrusive afternoon sun, while the aerial of his walkie-talkie pointed skywards.

'I'm Mario Conde,' he said to him.

'I was just leaving,' remarked the young man.

'We're on our way then.'

Later Conde would find out that this fresh-faced policeman was Inspector Palacios' official driver and that Manolo had chosen him because he was his exact counterpart in the world of automobiles, perhaps cloned in some special laboratory. This madman was not only capable of polishing the car beneath the pitiless sun at two in the afternoon, but he was also capable of making the trip between the *Biblioteca Nacional* and Finca Vigía in barely twenty minutes, each second of which cost Conde a lifetime of agony.

'We in a hurry?' he dared to ask as the driver negotiated his way around the *Fuente Luminosa* roundabout by dint of much blowing on his horn and shouting.

'Don't know, but just to be on the safe side . . .' he replied, stepping on the accelerator.

When he got out of the car in the parking space next to Finca Vigía, Conde felt his legs shaking and an overwhelming dryness burnt his mouth. For a couple of seconds he leant back against the car, waiting for his muscles to relax and his heart to regain its usual rhythm. Then he looked at the police driver. There was hatred, a lot of hatred, in Conde's expression.

'You fucking bastard,' he said, in a voice deep with feeling, and went towards the museum office.

He decided to walk back to the house along the tarmac drive. He knew it was three times further than the short-cut through the casuarina trees, but it was an easier climb. Anyway, he wasn't in a hurry. The combination of wine and the discovery of the police badge had scared sleep away and he now had a feeling that he would sleep little and badly, as had tended to happen of late. At his side, Black Dog mirrored the step of his master, without barking or moving away towards the trees.

As he was going up the last slope, skirting around the garages and the guest bungalow, he noticed that he must have left the side door to the drawing-room open.

He went up the six steps onto the concrete platform that went round the house and then the next six that led up to the front door. He put the key in the lock and glanced inside. The lamps were still alight; the clock, the bottle and glass were on the oriental rug; the Miró was on the main wall of the dining-room. Solitude was the only tangible presence, moving freely amid the memories of nights of plentiful alcohol and conversation spent in that very room, often preceded by the explosion of gunpowder and the joyful din of the two little bronze cannons, reserved for greeting the most special guests. Black Dog, in the doorway, sniffed towards the inside of the house, but when he tried to go in, Hemingway spoke to him.

'Heel, Black Dog . . . that's enough for today.' The animal stopped and looked up at his master. 'Here's your mat. Look after the house; you're a great dog,' he said, and stroked his head, gently pulling his ears.

He closed the front door and then the one

leading to the covered terrace with the pergola. He couldn't think how he could have forgotten to close it when he went on his rounds.

Blaming himself for this, he went over to the little wooden bar and poured himself a good measure of gin and drank it down in one go, as if he were swallowing some medicinal potion intended to quieten his nerves. He turned off all the lamps except the one nearest his room so he could see by its glow. When Miss Mary was away he preferred to sleep in his own room in order to ward off the feeling of neglect which a double bed, only half occupied, aroused in him. When he went into the room he unslung the Thompson from his shoulder and placed it next to his old walking-stick of *güira* wood, leaning it against the bookcase where he kept the various editions of his works. Having decided to return the machine gun to its place in the tower, he wanted to have it visible so as not to forget yet again to take it back.

More than half his bed was covered with newspapers, magazines and letters. He grabbed the bedspread by its edges to make a big bundle, which he dropped between the bed and the window that looked out onto the swimming pool. As if he were going to the gallows, he went into the bathroom and pissed a heavy, murky froth. After placing his .22 revolver on the edge of the wash basin he undressed, dropping his shirt and shorts between the bidet and the toilet. He took his striped pyjamas from the wooden hook, but only put on the pyjama trousers: it was too hot for the jacket. As he did every night, he got onto the scales and recorded his weight on the wall next to it: 2 Oct. '58: 220. It was the same weight he had been throughout the year, he noted with satisfaction.

Hemingway went back into the room and looked in the desk drawer for Ava Gardner's knickers and wrapped the revolver in them, placing it at the bottom of the first drawer, between boxes of bullets and a couple of commando knives. He went towards the end of the bed, but paused next to his faithful Royal portable, Arrow model. Next to it, under a lump of copper ore, were the last pages that he had written of that ill-fated novel that just wouldn't drop into place. With one of his sharpened pencils he jotted down the date on the last revised sheet of foolscap: 2 Oct. '58.

Then he looked at the bed, unsure if he wanted to get into it. The pleasant sensation of solitude had disappeared and a pervasive, icy feeling of unease ran though his body. He had spent his whole life surrounded by people whom, in one way or another, he had turned into a chorus of admirers. Crowds were his natural medium, and he had only done without them in the four activities he had to do alone, or at most with one companion: hunting, fishing, loving and writing (although in those years in Paris he had managed to write some of his best stories in cafes, surrounded by people, and more than one fishing trip on the high seas had turned into a wild party amongst the islands of the Gulf). But everything else had been part of the uproar his existence had become since his adolescence, when he first discovered how much he liked being the centre of attention, appearing as the leader and giving orders in the role of boss. Accompanied by a group of hedonists and acting as a prophet, he had attended the San Fermín Festival in Pamplona, where he showed Dos Passos how big his own balls were when he squared up to a magnificent bull and dared to touch its head. With men who admired him he'd joined in the Republican offensive in the Spanish Civil War, visited the frontline positions in order to make the film *Spanish Soil* and drunk his fill of wine, whisky and gin in the Hotel Florida, listening to the bombs falling upon Madrid. With his group of crooks he'd sailed for almost a year between the coves of the northern coast of Cuba, barely armed but well supplied with rum and ice, while claiming to be hunting for German submarines. With a band of experienced French guerrillas and two water bottles filled with whisky and gin he'd advanced towards the Nazi lines following the Allied landing in Normandy and participated with those tough *maquisards* in the heroic liberation of the Ritz Hotel, where he again drank his fill of wine, more whisky and more gin . . . The treacherous Martha Gellhorn, determined to report even their most intimate life and to describe him as hard-working but cold and repetitive in bed, said that his need for company was a sign of latent homosexuality. What a whore: it was she who would plead with him at the top of her voice to give it to her in the ass and to bite her nipples until she cried aloud with pleasure and pain.

Sitting on his bed, he looked once more into the darkness. The heat forced him to leave the window open, and he checked that he would only need to take a couple of steps and stretch out an arm in order to get hold of the Thompson. But not even this made him feel safe. So he stood up and went in search of his revolver, placing it on the bedside table on his side of the bed. Before putting it down, he sniffed the lace it had been wrapped in, but its original feminine perfume had already been overpowered by the manly stench of grease and gunpowder. Still, it was a lovely souvenir to have.

He let his head fall back against the pillow and his eyes focused on his dear old Mannlicher rifle, half-hidden by the magnificent presence of the enormous head of the African buffalo shot on the Serengeti Plain during his first African safari, in 1934. A sensation of warm relief ran through him as he contemplated the amazing head of the animal whose tracking and sacrifice had shown him the paralysing intensity of fear and helped him to accept the insignificance of death. That awareness had inspired *The Short Happy Life of Francis Macomber*. To kill while running the risk of dying is one of the apprenticeships indispensable for a man, he thought, and he was sorry that this expression, precisely as he had just formulated it, was not included in any of his stories of hunting, death and war.

With this authentic and beautiful phrase in his mind and the image of the African buffalo before his eyes, he started to read in an attempt to get to sleep. A couple of days before, he had started to look through an absurd and crazy novel by a certain J.D. Salinger, whose only claim to fame was having returned half crazy from the campaign in France, where he had served as a sergeant. The novel told the adventures of a rude, foul-mouthed young man who has made up his mind to run away from home, and who, just like a character from Twain but transported to a modern city in the north, begins to discover the world from his own very twisted perspective. The story was more than predictable, lacking the epic quality and greatness that he himself demanded of literature, and he only carried on reading it in search of the mysterious key that had turned this absurd book into a bestseller, and its author into the new revelation of his country's novel writing. Shows what a goddamn mess we're in, he said to himself, although without a great deal of conviction.

He wasn't aware of the moment at which, with his book resting on his chest and his glasses on his nose, he closed his eyes and fell asleep. It wasn't a deep sleep, because the light of consciousness remained switched on in his mind, like the reading light that he didn't get round to putting out. Wandering through that vague place between sleep and watchfulness, he had the impression that he was hearing the distant, insistent barking of Black Dog, when he opened his eyes. There in front of him, instead of the African buffalo, he found the blurry image of a man staring at him.

Conde certainly recognised that expression: he had seen it too often not to detect the triumphant sarcasm that pervaded it.

'So you've got something good for me,' he said with the voice of a man quite prepared to be amazed, as he walked next to Inspector Palacios.

'How do you know?'

'Just look at yourself in a mirror.' He paused beneath the areca palms that formed a small clump in front of the house and looked at Manolo.

'I think we can release the body for burial now,' announced the cop as he put his hand in his pocket. 'Look at this.'

He saw the bullet in the palm of Manolo's hand. It still had earth in the rifling marks and was dark grey in colour, a fact which meant nothing to Conde.

'There was further evidence in the earth. We found it this morning.'

'Just one? Wasn't he shot twice?'

'The other shot probably went straight through his body, and God knows where it ended up . . .'

'Maybe. And have they found out which weapon this bullet came from?'

'We're not certain, but Constable Fleites says it must be from a Thompson machine gun. You know, the guy's an expert in ballistics but he has been reduced in rank because of his drinking.'

'So they're now punishing drunken experts? Or perhaps they're expert drunkards?'

Manolo barely managed a smile.

'And Hemingway had a Thompson. Tenorio says he often used it to kill sharks when he went on fishing trips. But that's not all: we searched the inventories and the Thompson isn't among the weapons that were left at the Finca, nor was it among the things his widow took away after he killed himself. By the way, the lady took away all the valuable paintings . . .'

'But I'm sure I've seen that Thompson. No, the earth didn't swallow it up.'

'Look, that's not a bad idea: it's probably buried as well.'

'When someone wants to get rid of a weapon

they don't bury it. They throw it into the sea. And if you've got a yacht . . .'

'Amazing, Conde's as sharp as ever,' interrupted Manolo, with obvious scorn. 'But where the Thompson got to is no longer of any importance, and I think you're going to have to forget about your hunches. Listen to this: in the records of the secret police we found the case of a search for an FBI agent who disappeared in Cuba in 1958. The agent, a certain John Kirk, was attached to the US Embassy in Havana and was carrying out routine work here, nothing of importance. At least that's what his superiors said when he went missing, and it must be true, because he was almost sixty years old and he was lame. The fact is nothing more was heard of him, because when the revolution was won nobody took it upon themselves to continue looking for him.'

'Was the lame John Kirk lost on 2 October 1958, by any chance?'

Conde knew how to administer deadly sword thrusts, and he enjoyed seeing their devastating results: all the confidence of his former subordinate began to collapse as he grimaced. Manolo stared at Conde with his mouth half-open.

'What the hell are you . . . ?'

'That's what happens when you get smart with me,' smiled Conde, full of satisfaction. 'Look, Manolo, now I need you to help me, because I'm sure that I'm going to have other interesting things to tell you. Call up the director of the museum, I need to have another look round the house. But tell him that it's on one condition: he can't speak unless we ask him a question, OK?'

Manolo, with a mixture of amazement and admiration, watched as Conde went up the steps to the house and turned back to look at the gardens of the Finca, particularly the spot where a corpse, a bullet from a Thompson, and an FBI badge had been found. The mystery was heating up dangerously.

The Inspector came back with the director of the museum. Juan Tenorio did not seem happy with the situation and looked at the alleged boss of the operation who, according to his information, wasn't actually the boss of anything.

'Where was the training ring, exactly?' Conde asked him.

'Well, it was right over there, where the body was found.'

'And why weren't we told this?'

'Well,' repeated Tenorio, also deprived of his self-confidence, 'I didn't think . . .'

'You've got to be a bit more imaginative, pal,' Conde preached at him in a dogmatic tone of voice, applying to his form of address the Hemingway technique for drawing attention to the defects in his acolytes, before going on to forgive them later.

'It's all right, it doesn't matter now. Let's have a look inside.'

The director moved ahead and opened the door.

'What are you looking for, Conde?' Manolo whispered to him.

'I want to know what happened in this house on the 2nd and 3rd October 1958.'

While the director was opening the shutters, Conde, followed by Manolo, went over to the library.

'Look at this.' He pointed to the second shelf of the bookcase nearest to the door. Between *The*

Trap by Enrique Serpa and a biography of Mozart, the thick spine of a book bearing the red letters *The FBI Story* stood out. 'It was a subject that interested him, it seems he read it more than once. And look who wrote the Introduction: his old pal Hoover, the same person who ordered him to be kept under surveillance.' Turning back to the director, he said, 'I need to see Hemingway's passports and papers connected with the house. Receipts, invoices, taxes . . .'

'At once. The papers are right here,' he replied, moving over to a wooden drawer.

'Manolo, look for anything dated between the 2nd and 4th October 1958. If you want, tell Constable Fleites to give you a hand.'

'He can't.'

'What's the matter with him?'

'He was overjoyed at finding the bullet and he's in the bar down there knocking back the rum.'

'Where is that bar? I didn't see one.'

The director made two trips and on the long rolltop desk at the back of the library there were now two mounds of papers in cardboard files and manila envelopes all ready for him. Conde breathed in the pleasing smell of old paper.

'Please be careful with them. They're very important papers . . .'

'Sure,' said Conde. 'What about the passports?'

'They're in my office, I'll get them.'

Tenorio went out, and Manolo, clicking his tongue, sat down at the desk.

'You always fuck me around Conde – in the end it's always me who's got to search through the fucking files of papers and . . .'

Conde paid little attention to what he was saying. Looking at books, walls, objects, as if prompted by a scientific curiosity, he walked slowly out of the library. Through a window in the drawing-room he saw the director walking towards the museum offices in the former garage and quickly turned towards Hemingway's private bedroom. At the back, next to the bathroom, was the writer's wardrobe, which held his trousers and the hunting jackets he used in Africa and the United States, his fishing waistcoat, a thick military cape, and even an old bullfighter's outfit with gold braid and sequins, no doubt given to him by one of the famous bullfighters he'd admired so much. Below, set out in the perfect order of a re-created life, were the boots he'd worn for hunting, fishing and reporting the war on the European front. Everything smelt of lifeless cloth, cheap insecticide and neglect. Conde closed his eyes and focused on his sense of smell, ready to pounce: something was oozing skin and blood in his trunk of memories. Almost automatically he stretched out his hand towards a shoebox placed next to the wardrobe. Handkerchiefs, stained by time, revealed their freckly countenance from inside the box. Delicately, with trembling hands, he lifted the folded pieces of cloth by their edges and his heart missed a beat as his eyes fell upon the dark material: tucked in between the writer's old handkerchiefs quietly rested Ava Gardner's black knickers. Feeling like a desecrator of secret things, the ex-cop took out the knickers, and after looking at them for a moment against the light, imagining everything that they had once held within them, he put them into his pocket, replaced the box, closed the wardrobe and went into the adjoining bathroom.

As his breathing calmed down, Conde studied the dates and records of weight that Hemingway had noted down on the bathroom wall next to the scales. The parallel columns of figures were not in chronological order, and Conde had to look through them carefully before he found the one for 1958. When he found it, he began to go down the column that began in the month of August but broke off on 2 October 1958, when a weight of 220 pounds was recorded. Later entries related to the final months of 1959 and the first ones of 1960, during Hemingway's final stay at this house. Conde noticed how they showed that the end was in sight: the writer now weighed little more than 200 pounds, and in the final entries, made in July 1960, he was just 190 pounds. All Hemingway's real, personal drama was written on that wall, and it spoke more eloquently of his troubles than any of his novels, letters, interviews and gestures, for here it had been just him and his body, with no other witnesses than time and some indifferent, ominous bathroom scales, chronicling his approaching death.

Approaching footsteps roused Conde from his musings. With the most innocent expression in the world he poked his head out of the bathroom and saw the museum director with the passports in his hand.

'Where did he keep his firearms?' Conde asked.

'Here, next to the wardrobe he had a glass-fronted gun cabinet. The others were kept on the second floor of the tower, with lots of knives, and spears of the Masai tribe that he brought back from his safari there in '54.'

'The bastard was obsessed with weapons! And what about the Thompson? Was it kept there too?'

'He generally used to keep it there, in the tower. He had his hunting shotguns here, and his Mannlicher rifle, which always hung above the bookcase.'

'But I've seen that Thompson, I'm sure of it,' said Conde as he wracked his brains. 'Well, which passport relates to 1958?' he asked Tenorio, who placed the passports on the desk in the grotesque shadow of the huge African buffalo.

'This one,' he said eventually, holding out one of the passports to him. 'It starts in 1957.'

Conde checked through it page by page until he found what he was looking for: an exit stamp for Cuba dated 4 October 1958, together with an entry stamp, indicating arrival at Miami airport, Florida, the same day.

'Yes, he stopped writing on 2 October, weighed himself for the last time, and left on the 4th. What we need to find out now is what he did on the 3rd. And Manolo is going to tell us that.'

On the desk, Manolo had already separated out most of the files.

'These are documents of ownership and receipts, but from the 1940s,' he pointed out. 'Help me with these ones.'

The director and Conde walked over to him.

'What are you looking for?' enquired Tenorio.

'As I said, 3 October 1958 . . . Help him for a bit, I'm going out for a minute, I've got to have a smoke.'

Conde crossed the room and, before leaving the house, he looked once again at the drawing-room with its bullfight scenes and empty chairs, its little bar with the dried-up bottles, sterilised by time. He glanced over the dining-room with its hunting trophies and the table laid with notable items from the dinner service marked with the insignia of the Finca Vigía; he saw at the back, in the room in which Hemingway used to write, the foot of the bed where he would sleep off his drunken binges and have his siestas. Conde knew that he was coming to the end of something and he was preparing himself to bid farewell to the place. If his hunches continued to be as accurate as they had been in the past, it would be many years before he returned to this nostalgic, literary estate.

With the cigarette still unlit between his lips, Conde went down to the area of the garden where the fountain was situated and around which the police had excavated about thirty square metres. On the edge of the hole, leaning against the peeled trunk of an African pepper tree, Conde lit his cigarette and strained his imagination to picture what had existed there forty years before. The rings used to train fighting cocks in are usually round, like those for real fights, although they're generally confined within walls a metre high, often made of sacking attached to wooden stakes to form a circle about four or five metres in diameter. The one at Finca Vigía didn't have a roof, but it was shaded by the mango trees, the carolina tree and the African pepper trees, and the trainer and the occasional spectators could spend hour after hour there, untroubled by the sun. With his imagination now working flat-out, Conde pictured Toribio el Tuzao there, just as he remembered him on the day he had met him at an official cockpit. He was wearing a sleeveless T-shirt, standing inside the ring with a cockerel in his hand, provoking the other animal in order to get it worked up. The cockerels had their spurs covered with rags to avoid unnecessary injuries. Next to the ring, from behind a curtain of sacking, Hemingway would be watching the process in silence. Excitement showed in his face when Tuzao finally released the cockerel he had been holding, and the animals clashed with each other, raising their deadly spurs (though merely decorative for training), and scattering with their

wings the wood shavings covering the earth . . .
The wood shavings. Conde saw them shifting
between the claws of the cockerels and he
understood everything: they had buried the man in
the only place where the disturbed earth would not
arouse suspicion. The ring, once the earth was
returned to its place, would once again be covered
with wood shavings.

Relaxed, Conde went back to the house and
sat down on the steps leading to the front door. If
he knew anything about Hemingway, he knew that
Manolo would come out of the house with a piece
of paper dated 3 October 1958. So he was not
surprised when he heard the Inspector's voice as he
approached with a receipt in his hand.

'Here it is, Conde.'

'How much did he pay him?'

'Five thousand pesos . . .'

'An awful lot of money. Even for Hemingway.'

'Who was Calixto Montenegro?'

'A very strange employee at the Finca.
Hemingway sacked him that day, paid him some
compensation and, if I'm not very much mistaken,

put him on board the *Pilar* and took him to Mexico.'

'Why did they do that?'

'Because I believe that he was the only one present when the FBI agent was killed . . . although I'm sure that he wasn't the only one who saw how they buried him under the training ring.'

'But who killed the guy?'

'I still don't know that, although we can probably discover it right now. I've an idea, if you're not in a hurry and want to come with me to Cojímar.'

'Afternoon, Ruperto.'

'You here again?'

'Yeah. But the worst of it is that I've brought the police with me this time. Things are serious. Look, this is Inspector Palacios.'

'He's very thin to be an inspector,' said Ruperto, and smiled.

'Couldn't agree with you more,' replied Conde as he sat down on the same stone that he had occupied that morning. Ruperto was still leaning back against the tree, facing the landing-stage on the river, with his Panama hat fixed firmly on his head. It looked as though he hadn't moved from that place, as if their conversation had never been interrupted by Conde's departure. The number of hours that had elapsed could only be detected from looking at the cigar between Ruperto's fingers, which had been smoked as far as it would go, and from which there arose the stench of scorched grass.

'I knew you'd be back . . .'

'Was I a long time?' asked Conde, while he motioned Manolo to another stone nearby. The Inspector picked it up and carried it nearer the tree.

'Depends. For me time is very different. Look,' he said as he raised his arm, 'it's as if I were there on the other side, across the river.'

'And into the trees,' continued Conde.

'Yeah, right there, among the trees,' confirmed Ruperto. 'From over there lots of things look different, don't they?'

Conde agreed as he lit his cigarette. Manolo, now sitting on his stone, tried to make his emaciated buttocks as comfortable as he could, as he watched the old man and tried to figure out his friend's strategy.

'Well, Ruperto, this is how I see things from this side of the river: on the night of 2 October 1958 an FBI agent was killed at Finca Vigía. The man killed was John Kirk, in case his name interests you.'

Conde waited for some reaction in Ruperto, but he continued gazing at something far away, beyond the river, deep into the trees: perhaps he was looking at death itself.

'Hemingway left Cuba on the 4th, and the strange thing is that he broke off from a very important piece of work. He was never able to finish it later on. He left for the US, according to him to join his wife, who was already over there. But on the 3rd he sacked Calixto and paid him some compensation. He gave him five thousand pesos. A hell of a lot of money, wasn't it?'

Ruperto was feeling the heat. He took off his Panama and wiped his hand across his brow. He had huge hands, disproportionately so, covered in wrinkles and scars.

'The normal compensation would be wages for two, three months . . . and Calixto earned a hundred and fifty pesos . . . How much did you earn?'

'Two hundred. Raúl and I were the ones who earned most.'

'He really did pay well,' observed Manolo. To remain silent, relegated to the role of observer, had always exasperated him, but Conde had demanded total discretion from him, like back in the days when they were the cops in greatest demand at the Station, and the Old Man, the best head of investigations there had ever been on the island, always put them to work together and even allowed them certain liberties, in the interests of greater efficiency.

'This John Kirk was killed with two shots,' went on Conde, while he drew something on the earth, in front of his feet, with a little stick. 'With a Thompson machine gun. And Hemingway had a Thompson that has disappeared. It's not in the house, and Miss Mary didn't take it away after he killed himself. It was a weapon he was very fond of, because I think he even mentioned it in his novels. Do you remember that Thompson?'

'Yes,' the old man put his hat back on, 'it was the one he killed sharks with. I used it myself a couple of times.'

'Indeed. The very same. After he was dead, the agent was buried at the Finca, not just anywhere, but under the training ring, quite close to the house. They moved the wood shavings, dug the hole, threw the guy in, and his police badge, and covered him with earth. Then they watered the wood shavings so that nobody would realise that there was a body under there . . . And, if I'm not very much mistaken, this happened before daybreak on the 3rd, before the other employees got to the Finca.'

The fleeting smile that crossed the old man's face surprised Conde and made him wonder whether he was going down the right road or had got lost down one of the dark paths of the past, so he plunged further on to get to the bottom of things.

'I think that there were three or four men present at the burial, to get it over with quickly. And I also think that one of those people was responsible for killing that cop: Calixto Montenegro, Raúl Villaroy or their boss, Ernest Hemingway. But I wouldn't be surprised to find out that it was Toribio Tuzao who killed him . . . or you, Ruperto.'

Once again Conde waited for some reaction,

but the old man didn't move a muscle, as if he were somewhere where the words of the ex-cop, the heat of the afternoon, and the assaults of memory could not get through to him. Conde looked down and finished the drawing that he had made on the earth with a stick: it almost resembled a yacht, with two long fishing rods sticking out from the deck, sailing on a stormy sea.

'Then the *Pilar* played a part in the proceedings,' he said as he hit the earth with his stick.

Ruperto slowly looked down at the drawing.

'That doesn't look like it.'

'I failed art and handicraft in first grade. It's been a dreadful failing all my life . . . I didn't even learn how to make paper boats,' lamented Conde. 'But the *Pilar* really did set sail on the 3rd and took Calixto to Mexico. Hemingway didn't go on that trip because he had to prepare for his departure from Cuba the next day. But you did, because the boat was only skippered by one of you two. And someone from the Finca went along as a deck-hand. Was it Raúl, was it Toribio? I think it was Toribio, because Raúl would stay back to help his Papa. By the way, the Thompson disappeared on that trip. It's somewhere in the Gulf of Mexico, isn't it?'

And with his stick he drew an arc, stretching out from the yacht, into the stormy sea. Conde dropped the stick and looked at the old man, ready to listen. Ruperto's eyes remained fixed on the far bank of the river.

'You think you know the whole story?'

'No, Ruperto, I know a few things, I can imagine a few others, but I'd like to know some more. That's why I'm here: because you do know them. If not all, at least some . . .'

'And if it were true, come on, why should I tell you?'

Conde took out another cigarette and put it between his lips. He paused with his lighter in his hand.

'For several reasons: first, because I don't think you were the murderer; second, because you're a law-abiding citizen. When you could have sold the *Pilar*, you handed it over to the government to be kept at the museum. And that boat was worth several thousand dollars. With that money your life would have changed a lot. But, no, Papa's memory was more important for you. That's strange: you don't find it nowadays. It seems silly, but it's also beautiful, because it's an incredibly honourable gesture. And now we reach the third reason: Hemingway could have killed the agent, but it might not have been him. If he killed him and we say that he did it, his honour will be done for. Nowadays, people don't like guys like that: too much shooting, too many fights, too many heroics. What's more, even if you don't believe this, he played dirty tricks on a lot of people. If we say he's the murderer, it will fuck up his reputation. But perhaps it wasn't Hemingway, and in that case the arrogant guy whom people don't like did something that day that's worthy of our respect: he protected one of those who worked for him after he had killed an FBI agent and even hid the body at the Finca. Whatever the consequences, that would have been a nice gesture, wouldn't it? As I said to you earlier, I don't think it would be right to blame him for a murder committed by another person . . .'

Ruperto put the cigar stub between his lips

and shifted his back against the tree, apparently trying to find a better position for his elderly bones and his misgivings. A tell-tale moisture was beginning to appear in the depth of his wrinkles. Conde decided to play his final card and he increased his bet to double or quits. But first he lit his cigarette.

'What happened on the night of 2 October '58 was a disaster for Hemingway. I don't know if you are aware that in his last years he used to say that the FBI were after him. The doctors believed that this was a figment of his imagination, a kind of persecution mania. And in order to cure him they gave him twenty-five electroshocks. For fuck's sake!' exclaimed Conde without being able to help it. 'First they gave him fifteen, then another ten. The doctors wanted him to forget the persecution mania that was driving him crazy, and all they managed to do was to fry his brain, and then they went on to stuff him full of pills . . . They gave him a living death. Hemingway couldn't write again, because along with the mania they removed part of his memory, and you can't write without a memory. Hemingway was lots of things, but above all he was a writer. In short: they screwed up his life. And that's very sad, Ruperto. As far as we know, Papa didn't have cancer or any life-threatening illness. But they had castrated him. He, who always wanted to show that he had balls, and who even showed them so that people could see that he had them, ended up castrated in here,' and Conde slapped his forehead with the palm of his hand, twice, three times, with force, with rage, until it hurt him. 'And without them he couldn't live. That's why he shot himself in the head, Ruperto, for no other reason. And that shot started to come out of the barrel of his gun on the night of 2 October 1958 . . . And if it wasn't him who killed that FBI agent, he really had to pay a high price to protect the person who did. Isn't that so Ruperto?'

Conde knew that his sword had cut mercilessly into the flesh of Ruperto's memory. And he wasn't in the least surprised when he noticed tears flowing from the corners of Ruperto's eyes, between those long, sweaty furrows. But the old man wiped them dry with his hand, still ready to put up a fight.

'Papa had leukaemia. That's why he killed himself.'

'Nobody has proved he had leukaemia.'

'He was losing weight. He got very thin.'

'His weight dropped to 155 pounds. He looked like a corpse.'

'Because of the illness . . . He got as thin as that?'

'He received twenty-five electroshocks, Ruperto, and thousands of pills. If it wasn't for all of that he'd probably still be alive, like you, like Toribio. But they screwed him up, and all that he needed then was to be landed with the murder of this dead man. The FBI really were after him. Their boss hated him and even suggested once that Hemingway was queer.'

'That's a lie, for God's sake!'

'Fine. Shall we save him or shall we sink him, Ruperto?'

The old man dried again the tears that were running down his face, this time with a weary movement. Conde felt like a wretch: did he have any right to deprive an old man of the best memories of his life? It was so that he wouldn't have to do things like this that he had stopped being a policemen.

'For me, Papa was the greatest person in the world,' said Ruperto, his voice now old. 'Since I first met him, right up to today, he's provided me with a living, and I'm deeply grateful.'

'You should be grateful, no doubt about it.'

'I don't know who killed the bastard who got into the Finca,' he said, without looking at them; he was talking as if he was addressing something in the distance, perhaps God. 'I never asked. But when Toribio knocked at my door about three in the morning, and said to me, "Come on, Papa sent me to get you," I went with him to the Finca. Raúl and Calixto were digging the hole and Papa held his large torch in his hand. He looked worried, but he wasn't nervous, there's no doubt about that. And he knew everything that had to be done.

'"We had a problem, Ruperto. But I can't tell you anything more. That clear?"

'"No need to say anything, Papa."

'He didn't say anything to Toribio either, but I think that he did tell Raúl about it. Raúl was like a real son to him. And I know that Calixto knew what happened that night.

'"Help to dig the hole."

'Toribio and I grabbed the shovels. Later, between Calixto and me, who were the strongest, we lifted the guy up. He weighed a ton. He was lying wrapped up in a bedspread at the door to the library. We got him out the best we could and we dropped him into the hole. Papa then threw the guy's badge in after him.

'"Raúl and Toribio, cover him up and reassemble the training ring. Hurry up, it's getting light and Dolores will soon be here. Calixto and Rupert, come with me."

'The three of us went back to the house. There was a bloodstain that was already drying where we had picked up the body.

'"Ruperto, clean that up, I've got to talk to Calixto."

'I started to clean up the blood and it was a

hell of a job getting rid of every trace. But I managed it. Meanwhile, Papa and Calixto were talking in the library, very quietly. I saw Papa give him some money and documents.

'"Finished doing that, Rupert? Fine, come here. Get the Buick straight away and take Calixto and Toribio with you. Set out in the *Pilar* and take Calixto to Mérida and then come back. And throw this into the sea."

'Papa picked up the Thompson and looked at it for a moment. He was reluctant to get rid of it. It was his son, Gigi's, favourite weapon.

'"I'll have to think up some story to tell Gigi."'

'Hell, that's it,' exclaimed Conde, 'I saw the Thompson in a photo. Hemingway's son was holding it in his hands.'

'It was small, easy to handle,' confirmed Ruperto.

'Go on, please.'

'Papa wrapped it up in a tablecloth, along with a black pistol and he gave the bundle to Calixto.

'"Off you go, it'll soon be light."

'He patted me here, on the back of the neck, and shook Calixto's hand and said something to him that I couldn't hear.

'"The bastard deserved it, Ernesto."

'Calixto was the only one of us who called him Ernesto.

'"Your dream is going to come true. Enjoy Veracruz. I warn you that if I fall in love with a Cuban girl . . ."

'That's what Papa said to him. When we left, Raúl and Toribio had already finished, and the three of us went off in the Buick. I did what he asked me to do: I took Calixto to Mérida. On the way, Calixto threw the Thompson and the pistol into the sea, and the tablecloth stayed floating on the surface until we lost it from sight. When I got back there the following night and went to the Finca to take back the Buick, Raúl told me that Papa had already left for the airport, but that he had left a message for Toribio and me.' Ruperto paused and threw his cigar butt in the direction of the river. 'The message said that he loved us as if we were his own sons and that he trusted us because we were men . . . Papa said things like that that filled you with pride, didn't he?'

The Masai also used to say that a man on his own isn't worth anything. But the most important thing that they had learnt after centuries of living on the dangerous plains of their country is that a man, without his spear, is completely worthless. Those Africans, ancestral hunters and furious runners, moved about in groups, avoided fights whenever they could, and slept clinging onto their spears, often with their hunting knives at their waists, since in this way they believed they gained the protection of the god of the grasslands. The picture of men talking around a campfire beneath a black and starless sky, flashed like lightning across his mind. He instantly passed from dreaming to consciousness, and when he managed to focus his gaze through the grimy lenses of his spectacles he discovered that the unknown man held Ava Gardner's black knickers and the .22 calibre revolver in his hand.

The intruder remained motionless, staring at him, as if he couldn't comprehend that Hemingway was capable of opening his eyes and looking at him. He was as big and thickset a man as himself, almost the same age, but he was breathing heavily, perhaps out of fear or perhaps because of the weight of his huge belly. He was wearing a black, narrow-brimmed hat, dark suit and tie, with a white shirt. He didn't need the badge for anyone to guess his line of work. Realising that the intruder was a cop and not a common robber came as something of a relief to Hemingway, but he felt humiliated that he had initially been afraid.

Still lying on his bed, he took off his spectacles to clean them with the sheet.

'You'd better keep still,' said the man, who had managed to unwrap the .22. 'I don't want any problems. No problems, please.'

'Sure about that?' Hemingway asked, putting on his spectacles again. He sat up in bed and tried to look calm. The man took a step backwards, with some difficulty. 'You invade my house and then say you don't want problems.'

'I just want my badge and my pistol. Tell me where they are and I'll leave.'

'What are you talking about?'

'Don't play dumb with me, Hemingway. I was drunk, but not that drunk . . . I lost them somewhere round here. And tell that goddamn dog to shut up.'

The man was getting worked up and Hemingway realised this increased his danger.

'I'm going to get up,' he said and held up his hands.

'Go on, shut that animal up.'

He put on the moccasins that were next to his bed and the man moved aside, still with the revolver in his hand, to let him go through to the drawing-room. As he passed by Hemingway smelt the acid stench of sweat and fear that the alcohol fumes the man was breathing out couldn't mask. Although he preferred not to look towards the bookcase in the corner, he was certain that the Thompson was still in its place, but he didn't think it necessary to go over to it. He opened the drawing-room window and whistled to Black Dog. The dog, who was also on edge, wagged his tail when he heard him.

'It's OK, Black Dog . . . it's OK. Now shut the fuck up: you've shown me what a good dog you are.'

The animal, still growling and with his ears pricked up, stood up on his hind-legs against the edge of the window.

'That's right, nice and quiet,' Hemingway added and stroked his head.

When he turned around, the FBI agent was looking at him scornfully. He seemed calmer and that was better.

'Give me my badge and my pistol and I'll go. I don't want problems with you . . . do you mind if I . . . ?'

And he pointed with the revolver to the little bar situated between two armchairs.

'Help yourself.'

As he went over to the bar Hemingway noticed that he was limping with his right leg. With the

revolver in his hand, he managed to uncork the gin
and pour himself half a glass. He drank a fair amount
of it.

'I love gin.'

'Just gin?'

'Gin as well as other things. But today I
overdid it with the rum. You start drinking and
before you know it . . .'

'Why did you come to my house?'

The man smiled. He had large teeth, crooked
and stained with tobacco.

'Just a routine call. We come here from time
to time, we have a look around, we check who your
guests are, we write a report. It was all so calm
here today that I took it into my head to jump over
the fence . . .'

Hemingway felt a wave of indignation that
swept away any remnants of the fear that he had
felt in bed.

'But what the hell . . . ?'

'Don't get worked up, Hemingway. It's
nothing to make a fuss about. Let's put it this way
so you understand what I'm saying: you like

communists and we don't. In France, in Spain and even in the US you've got lots of communist friends. And here as well. Your doctor, for instance. And this country's at war and when there's war communists can be very dangerous. At times they don't stick their noses in, but they're always on the look-out, waiting for their opportunity.'

'What's that got to do with me?'

'Nothing so far, I agree. But you talk a great deal and we know that you've given them money, haven't you?'

'What I do with my money . . .'

'Hold on, hold on, I didn't come here to argue about your money or your political inclinations. I want my badge and my gun.'

'I haven't seen them.'

'You must have seen them. I lost them between the fence at the bottom of the garden and the swimming pool. I've already looked all over for them but there's no sign. It must have been when I jumped over the fence . . .'

'I'm sorry. I haven't got anything of yours. Now give me my revolver and leave.'

The man had another swig, put his glass down on top of a bookcase and took out a cigarette. He lit it, blew the smoke out through his nose and coughed. His eyes began to water and he seemed tearful when he spoke again.

'You're going to land me in it, Hemingway. In December I retire with thirty years' service and an allowance for physical incapacity: some bastard fucked up my leg and look how I've ended up . . . I can't say that I lost my badge while I was climbing into your property, to say nothing of my gun. Got it?'

'They're going to find out anyway. When I tell the journalists about it . . .'

'Listen, don't break my balls like that.'

'But it's all right for you to knee me there and even land a few kicks, is it?'

The man shook his head, denying this. He spoke and smoked without removing the cigarette from his mouth.

'Look, Hemingway, I'm nothing, I don't exist, I'm just a number in a huge squad. Don't make life difficult for me, please. It's not my fault there are reports on you. My job's to keep an eye on you, nothing else. On you and fifteen other crazy Americans like you who wander about this city and who like communists.'

'This is an outrage . . .'

'OK. It's an outrage. Go to Washington and tell my big boss that, or the president himself. It was them who gave me the order. And not directly to me, of course. Between them and me there are a thousand bosses . . .'

'How long have you had me under surveillance?'

'I don't know . . . since just after 1930, I think. I started two years ago, when they posted me to the embassy in Havana. And I curse the day I agreed to come to this goddamn awful country. Look how I'm sweating, and the humidity has played hell with my knee and the rum makes me lose my wits . . . With all the money you've got, why the devil did you decide to come here?'

'What did you say in your reports on me?'

'Nothing that wasn't common knowledge,' he finally removed the cigarette from his lips and had another drink to empty the glass. 'Where can I put my ash?'

Hemingway moved over to the bookcase beneath the window, thinking it grotesque that the man should dirty the beautiful Venetian glass ashtray, a gift from his old friend Marlene Dietrich. Then he threw it over to the agent, but the man, despite his age and size, moved quickly and caught it.

'Thanks,' he said.

'You didn't answer my question about what you said about me,' he insisted.

'Please, Hemingway . . . You know Hoover doesn't like you, don't you?' The man seemed tired. He looked up and saw that it was 1.50 on the clock on the wall. 'I said what everybody knows: who comes to your house, what goes on there when there are parties, how many of your friends are communists and how many might be. Nothing else. The whole business of your drinking and the seamy side of your private life were already in your file when I came to Cuba. Anyway, I'm too drunk to talk about my colleagues,' and he tried to smile.

The first symptom that his blood pressure had risen was usually the stabbing pain in his temples that was capable of producing, in a flash, a massive heaviness at the back of his head, right at the base of his skull. There then followed a burning sensation in his ears. But he had never experienced it so intensely before. What was this seedy side of his private life the man was referring to? What could those gorillas, who marched over the face of the earth with impunity, know about him?

'What are you talking about?'

'Wouldn't it be better if you just gave me my badge and my gun, and I could leave and we could all go about our own business? I think so . . .'

He thought it over for a moment, and made his mind up.

'I didn't see your gun. Your badge was beside the pool, under the pergola.'

'Of course,' smiled the man, 'I should have known. I sat down for a while to have a cigarette there. My knee was hurting . . . And wasn't my damn gun there as well?'

'I'll give it to you if you tell me what's written in that file.'

The agent stubbed out the cigarette on the bottom of the ashtray which he put on the carpet.

'For God's sake, Hemingway. Stop screwing me around and give me my badge.' His voice had taken on a hardness and his eyes were full of hatred and despair.

'Your badge in return for information!' he shouted, and Black Dog began to bark again.

'Shut that fucking dog up. The watchman will hear.'

'The information!'

'You goddamn . . .' the man raised the revolver and pointed it at his chest. 'Shut the dog up or I'll shut it up once and for all!'

'If you kill the dog you won't get out of here alive. So you'd better start talking!'

The man was sweating so much the sweat was running down his face. Still pointing the gun at the dog, he moved his hat back on his head and wiped his left hand across his face.

'Don't be stupid, Hemingway, I can't tell you that.'

'Well I won't give you your badge. And I'm going to call the watchman.'

Black Dog was still barking when he took a

step towards the window. At that moment he felt his head would explode and he wasn't able to think. He just knew that he had to exploit the agent's situation in order to force him to talk. The agent, surprised by the movement, hesitated a moment before moving into action. He took three paces forward and stretched out one of his arms to grab Hemingway by the shoulder. When he finally managed to get hold of him, he hauled him backwards. But Hemingway had already seized hold of one of the solid silver Spanish candlesticks and, with the impetus of this movement, he spun round and hit the man on the neck. It was a good blow, heavy, but he didn't land it squarely. The man moved back, with his left hand on the place where he had received the blow and his right arm stretched out, trying to aim the .22 at Hemingway.

'What the hell are you playing at? I'm going to kill you, you filthy faggot!'

The first shot rang through the house and the agent took a step to his left, holding his hand to his abdomen. Drunkenly, he attempted to regain his balance in order to get Hemingway in the sights of his revolver again. Just as he managed to get his aim, there came a second shot. It seemed friendlier, as if it were just pushing him. He fell on one side, his eyes open, his free hand clutching his stomach, the revolver in the other.

At the door of the room Calixto lowered the Thompson. At his side, Raúl was pointing a shiny black gun, still smoking, and trembling in his hand. Raúl then lowered the weapon, while Calixto went over to the collapsed man. With his boot he trod on the hand that still clutched the .22 and with the other foot he kicked the gun away.

'You all right, Papa?' Raúl went towards him.

'Don't know, I think so.'

'Sure you're all right?'

'I said I was. Where did that gun come from?'

'It must belong to that guy. Calixto and I found it.'

'This bastard was going to kill you, Ernesto,' observed Calixto.

'You think so?'

'Yes, I think so,' and he leant the Thompson against the wall.

ॐ ॐ

'Why didn't you want to come to the station?'

'I don't like the station anymore.'

'Haven't you ever been back?'

'Not once,' confirmed Conde as he bent over the stove. He saw that the coffee was almost ready. 'I'm not a cop any more and I have no intention of being one again.'

Sitting at the table, Inspector Manuel Palacios was fanning himself with an old newspaper. Although he had insisted, Conde absolutely refused to talk to the head of investigations, but he did agree to Manolo taking him home.

With very deliberate movements, Conde took a large china cup, put in a precise quantity of sugar and then poured in the coffee. He stirred it with the seriousness of an expert and poured it back into the coffeepot. Then he served his friend with some in a small cup and put his back into the large cup.

He breathed in the warm aroma of the infusion and felt the familiar pleasurable sensation on his palate. Finally, he poured a small quantity of the liquid into a bowl and called his dog, who was dozing beneath the table.

'Come on, Garbage, coffee.'

The animal stretched and moved towards the bowl. It put its tongue into it and then removed its snout.

'Blow on it first, Garbage, it's hot.'

'Instead of giving him coffee you should give him a bath.'

'He prefers coffee. It's good, isn't it?'

'Damn good,' replied Manolo. 'Where do you get such good coffee from, Conde?'

'It's Dominican. A friend of the Old Man, who became a great friend of mine as well, sends it to me. Freddy Ginebra. Don't you know him?'

'No, I don't.'

'Strange. Everyone knows Freddy Ginebra . . . Well, what do you intend to do?'

'I'm not really sure yet. There are things I don't think we're ever going to find out. Anyway

I want to talk to Toribio and with Raúl Villaroy's son. They probably know something . . .'

'They don't know anything. Neither Hemingway nor Calixto nor Raúl said what happened that night. According to my reckoning they were the only ones who knew the whole story. And all three of them are dead,' Conde smoked and looked out of the open window. 'We already know all that can be known . . .'

'As far as I'm concerned it's clear that Calixto was the one who killed him. If not, they wouldn't have taken him off to Mexico.'

'I'm not so certain. Anything could have happened there. Calixto probably only saw what happened, or the FBI were after him and not Hemingway . . . Anyway, with the body hidden away, why bother sending Calixto to Mexico? It could have been a smoke screen . . . No, there's something strange in all of this and I can't be certain that it was Calixto.'

'What's wrong with you, Conde? Why don't you want to see the truth? Look, Hemingway got Calixto out of Cuba to protect him. He was also capable of doing things like that, wasn't he?' Manolo didn't take his eyes off Conde. 'And if he saved Calixto, he behaved like a friend.'

'In that case, why get everybody involved? We thought only Hemingway and Calixto were at the Finca, but it turns out that suddenly Raúl and Toribio were there, and then they sent for Ruperto. Isn't that strange? And the second bullet, where the hell's the second bullet? Did it come from the Thompson as well?'

'Conde, Conde . . .' Manolo started to object.

'And what if the second bullet didn't come from a Thompson? And what if Hemingway was the one who killed him and got Calixto out for some other reason? I don't know, to stop him talking . . .'

'For God's sake, you really want to look for difficulties. Look, what I can't get my head around is what the hell that FBI agent was doing in the house. Keeping him under surveillance is one thing, attacking him is quite another . . . And Hemingway was no jerk whom they could pressurise just like that. And I can't think of any reason why they didn't throw the badge in the sea either . . .'

Manolo took a cigarette out of Conde's packet and stood up. He moved towards the door of the kitchen, which opened onto the porch and the yard, shaded by an old mango tree.

'I'd love to see the fifteen missing pages from the FBI file,' Manolo breathed out the smoke and turned round. 'I don't know why, but I think that the key to everything that happened that night lies there.'

'There are secrets that can kill . . . And that one killed at least two men: the agent and Hemingway. Everyone lost out.'

'Well, well . . . So you don't think he's so bad now?'

'Don't know. I have to wait for the tide to go back out.'

'You know something? I reread the short story you mentioned. "Big Two-Hearted River".'

'And . . . ?'

'It's a strange story, Conde. Nothing happens yet you feel that lots of things are happening. He doesn't say what you have to imagine.'

'He knew how to do that. The old story of

the iceberg. Remember? Seven parts hidden beneath the water, just one part visible, on the surface . . . Like now, isn't it? When I discovered how well he did it, I started to imitate him.'

'What are you writing now?'

Conde took two more drags on his cigarette, and felt his fingers getting hot. He glanced at the cigarette end for a moment and threw it out of the window.

'The story of a cop and a queer who become friends.'

Manolo went back to the kitchen. He smiled.

'Fuck you, in advance, for that,' said Conde.

'OK, OK. Everyone writes about what he can and not about what he wants to,' agreed the other.

'You going to close the case?'

'Don't know. There are things we don't know, but I don't think we're ever going to know them, are we? And if I close it, it's proof that it happened. And if it happened, the shit's going to fly. Irrespective of whether it was Calixto or Hemingway who did it, there's going to be one bloody awful fuss. And I still think that after forty years, who cares about a dead man?'

'You thinking what I'm thinking?'

'I'm thinking that if when we've gone through all of this we don't know who killed him, or why, and we can't accuse anyone of it, and the body hasn't been claimed by anyone . . . Isn't it better just to forget all about that bag of bones?'

'What about your bosses?'

'I can probably bring them round to this. What do you think?'

'If the boss were the Old Man you could. Chief Rangel seemed tough, but he had his soft spot. I could have persuaded him.'

'So what do you think?'

'Wait here.'

Conde went to his room and came back with the biography of Hemingway he had been reading.

'Look at this photo,' and he handed the book to Manolo. Hemingway appeared in profile, standing, with a curtain of trees in the background. His hair and his beard were completely white, and his gingham shirt seemed as if it had been lent to him by another Hemingway, stouter than the one in the photo. His body had shrunk, his shoulders had drooped and narrowed. He seemed to look in thoughtful silence at something outside the photo, and on seeing the picture Manolo received a disturbing impression of veracity. The picture was that of an old man, and it hardly evoked the man who had indulged in and enjoyed violence. The caption indicated that the photo had been taken in Ketchum, before his final stay at the clinic, and it was one of the last photos ever taken of the author.

'What can he have been looking at?' asked Manolo.

'He was looking across the river, and into the trees,' replied Conde. 'He was seeing himself, without an audience, without any disguises, without any lights. He was seeing a man overcome by life. A month later he shot himself.'

'Yes, he was washed up.'

'No, on the contrary: he was free of the character he'd invented for himself. That's the real Hemingway, Manolo. That's the same guy who wrote "Big Two-Hearted River".'

'Shall I tell you what I'm going to do?'

'No, don't tell me,' Conde interrupted vehemently, waving his hand. 'That's the hidden part of the iceberg. Let me imagine it.'

The sea formed an unfathomable hostile stain, and only when it broke on the rocks was its black monotony modified by the fleeting crest of the waves. In the distance, two timid lights signalled the presence of fishing-boats, engaged in the fisherman's eternal challenge to harvest sustenance from the sea.

Sitting on the wall, Conde, Skinny and Rabbit were polishing off their supplies of rum. After devouring the chicken in garlic, the stew of sweet potato with bitter orange juice, the bowls of rice and the mound of fruit fritters in syrup prepared by Josefina, Conde had insisted that they go to Cojímar if they wanted to hear the whole story of the death of the FBI agent at Finca Vigía. Rabbit had asked his youngest brother to lend him the shiniest and flashiest 1956 Chevrolet Bel Air in Cuba. The miracle of the transformation of this antique, reborn from a heap of scrap metal and now valued at several thousand dollars, was due to the painstaking endeavour of the younger Rabbit, who had come into the possession of the cash needed to buy and embellish it in the six months or so that he had been running a bakery charging dollars, that seemed more like an inexhaustible gold mine.

Between them, Conde and Rabbit had lifted Carlos out of his wheelchair to get him up on the seafront wall and then, carefully, they moved his useless legs until they were dangling over it. The few lights visible in the town were behind them, beyond Hemingway's green bust, and the three of them felt that it was pleasant being there, looking out to sea alongside the Spanish watchtower, enjoying what breeze there was that night as they listened to Conde's story and drank rum straight out of the bottle.

'And what's going to happen now?' asked Rabbit, possessor of an unassailable logic, always anxious for answers of a similarly unassailable logic.

'Fuck all,' said Conde, summoning up the last

vestiges of his coherence, on the point of being drowned in alcohol.

'That's the best thing about this story,' said Skinny Carlos after draining the final drops from the second bottle. 'It's as if nothing had ever happened. There was no dead man, no killer, nothing. I like that . . .'

'But Hemingway doesn't seem the same to me now . . . somehow.'

'It's only right that he should seem different to you, Conde,' chipped in Skinny. 'After all, the guy was a writer and that's what matters to you; you're also a writer, not a cop, not a detective, not a bloody salesman. A writer, all right?'

'No, you idiot, I'm not so sure. Remember there are lots of kinds of writers,' and he began to count off on as many fingers as he could muster, 'good writers and bad writers, writers with dignity and writers without dignity, writers who write and those who say that they write, writers who are bastards and those who are honourable people . . .'

'And in which category do you place Hemingway? Come on!' Skinny wanted to know.

Conde uncorked the third bottle and took a short swig.

'I think he was a bit of all of them.'

'What gets me about him is that he only saw what interested him. Take this, for instance,' said Rabbit, and he turned to face the town. 'He said that it was a fishing village. Fuck him: nobody in Cuba says that *this* is a fishing *village*, and that's why Santiago is anything but a fisherman from Cojímar.'

'That's true as well,' pronounced Carlos. 'The guy didn't understand a damn thing. Or else he didn't care if he understood or not. Conde, do you know if he ever fell in love with a Cuban girl?'

'That's something I haven't found out.'

'And he still attempted to write about Cuba?' Rabbit seemed over-excited. 'What an old fraud . . .'

'Literature is one big lie,' concluded Conde.

'He's talking shit now,' interjected Skinny Carlos, and put a hand on his friend's shoulder.

'Well. I want you all to know,' continued Conde, 'I'm going to ask to join the Cuban Hemingwayians.'

'What the hell's that?' inquired Carlos.

'It's one of the two thousand possible and

accredited ways of bullshitting, but I like it: there are no bosses, nor rules, nor anyone to keep tabs on you and you come in and go out when you feel like it.'

'If that's what it is, I like it as well,' concluded Rabbit. 'I think I'm going to become a member too. Long live the Cuban Hemingwayians!'

'Hey, Conde,' Skinny looked at his friend, 'but in all this fuss you forgot to find out about one thing . . .'

'What's that, you old sonofabitch?'

'Ava Gardner's knickers.'

Conde looked Skinny straight in the eyes.

'I thought you knew me better.'

And he smiled, while with one hand he felt in the back pocket of his trousers, raising one buttock from the wall. With the exaggerated gestures of a cheap conjuror, he took out the lacy black material, the same stuff that once caressed the most private parts of one of the most beautiful women in the world. He opened the knickers with his hands, as if he were hanging them on a clothes line, so that his friends could observe the size, the shape, the transparent texture of the garment, and could imagine for themselves, feverishly, the living flesh that had once occupied that space.

'You stole them?' Skinny's admiration was boundless, as was his erotic hunger. He stretched out one of his hands and took hold of the knickers in order to feel between his fingers, close to his eyes, the warmth of the fabric of desire.

'You're bloody amazing, Conde,' Rabbit said to him and smiled.

'I had to get something out of this story, didn't I? Give them to me, Skinny,' he asked. His friend gave him back the piece of material. Delicately, Conde took hold of the elastic waistband and opened them with both hands and then lifted it up to his head: next he put them on his head as if they were a beret. 'This is the best crown of laurel leaves that any writer ever wore. This is my Phrygian cap.'

'When you get fed up with screwing around with them lend them to me,' demanded Rabbit, but Conde didn't seem to have any intention of removing his headgear.

'Give me the rum,' he asked, and he had another drink.

'Careful, you're already plastered,' Rabbit warned him.

From the distance, one of the lit-up fishing boats was approaching the shore.

'I wonder if they've caught anything?' said Skinny.

'I bet they have,' affirmed Conde. 'Unless they're hopeless cases, like us . . .'

In silence they watched the manoeuvring of the boat, whose engine was coughing intermittently, as if about to choke on its own phlegm. It slowly moved past them and made its way to the jetty in the river.

'I can't even remember how long it's been since I last came to Cojímar,' Skinny Carlos said at last.

'It's as strange a place as it ever was,' observed Conde. 'It's as if time stood still here.'

'The bloody awful thing about it is that it doesn't ever stand still, Conde,' interjected Rabbit with his imperturbable dialectic and feeling for history. 'The last time that we all came here together, Andrés was with us. Do you remember?'

'Pass me the rum,' asked Conde, 'I'm going to have a swig for our friend Andrés,' and he drank a devastating quantity.

'He went up north seven years ago.' Skinny took the bottle which Conde passed to him. 'Seven years is a long time. I don't know why he doesn't want to return yet.'

'I do,' affirmed Rabbit. 'In order to be able to live on the other side,' and he pointed to the sea, 'he needed to tear himself away from the life he left on this side.'

'You really think so?' cut in Carlos, 'and how's he going to live deprived of his life over here? No, Rabbit, no . . . Look, a moment ago I was imagining that Andrés could be over on the other side, looking out to sea just like us, and thinking about us. That's what friends are for: to remember each other, aren't they?'

'That would be great,' said Conde, 'and the funny thing is that it might be true.'

'I remember that bastard every day,' assured Carlos.

'I only remember him when I get drunk, like now,' said Rabbit. 'You can put up with things better that way. Sleeping or drunk . . .'

Conde leant forward, looking for a bottle they'd already drained dry.

'There,' he said to Skinny. 'Give me that empty litre bottle.'

'What do you want it for?' Carlos was apprehensive about his friend's alcoholic impulses. Conde looked out to sea.

'I also think that Andrés is on the other side, looking towards us. And I want to send him a letter. Give me that fucking bottle.'

With the bottle between his knees and a cigarette between his lips, Conde looked in his pockets for a bit of paper. All that he found was the packet with a couple of cigarettes still knocking around in it. He put the cigarettes in his pocket and, controlling the trembling of his hands, carefully tore it open until he had a rectangular piece of paper. Leaning on the wall, trying to get some light to see by, he began to write on the paper, while he read aloud the words that he was inscribing: 'To Andrés, somewhere in the north: you bastard, we're remembering you here. We still love you and I think that we're always going to love you', and he paused, with his ballpoint pen resting on the paper. 'Rabbit says that time doesn't stand still, but I think that's a lie. But if it is true, we hope that you still love us, because there are some things that shouldn't be lost. And if they do get lost, then we really are in a fucking mess. We've lost almost everything, but we've got to save what we can. It's night here, and we're all as drunk as hell, because we're drinking rum in Cojímar: Skinny who's no longer skinny, Rabbit who's no longer an official chronicler, and me, who's no longer a cop. And what about you, what are you or aren't you now? We send you our love, and some more for Hemingway if you see him over there, because we're now members of the Cuban Hemingwayians. When you receive this message, return the bottle, but make sure it's full.' Mario Conde signed the letter, then passed it to Carlos and Rabbit, who appended their signatures. With immense care, Conde rolled up the paper and put it inside the container. Then he took Ava Gardner's knickers from his head and began to put them inside the bottle.

'You've gone crazy,' protested Rabbit.

'That's what friends are for, aren't they?' commented Conde as he forced the material down into the belly of the bottle.

'Couldn't agree more,' seconded Skinny Carlos.

'It's bound to reach him on his birthday,' elaborated Rabbit, after taking a long swig of rum.

When the garment was inside, Conde stuck the cork deep into the neck of the bottle, and banged it with the flat of his hand so that the seal would be tight.

'It's going to get there,' affirmed Conde. 'I'm sure this message is going to get there.' And he took a long drink from the other bottle of rum, seeking the relief of oblivion.

Snorting alcoholic fumes from his last swig and without releasing his grip on the bottle, Conde struggled to get up and finally managed to stand on the wall. He looked out to the infinite sea and saw the hostile bed of rocks against which all the dreams and sorrows of a man could be smashed.

He took another drink to oblivion, and shouted with all the strength in his lungs:

'Adiós, Hemingway!'

Then he drew back his arm to gain momentum and flung the bottle out to sea. The epistolary container, heavy with the nostalgia of those three shipwrecked men, remained floating near the coast, shining like a priceless diamond, until a wave engulfed it and took it out to the dark zone where it's only possible to see things through the eyes of memory and desire.

Mantilla, Summer 2000